Refuse
To
Sink

Refuse
To
Sink

D. C Garriott

Copyright © 2012
D.C Garriott
All rights reserved.

Refuse To Sink is a work of Fiction. No use of this work with out authors permission aloud. Any resemblance to any living person is a coincidence.

Copyright © 2012 by Danielle Garriott-Caswell

Cover Photo: © Amy Horn

Musical Influences used in this book are not owned by D.C.
Marry Me : Train (2009)
She is Love: Parachute (2009)
A Drop in the Ocean: Ron Pope (2011)

Maine information obtained for the book:
www.Maine.gov
www.Visitmaine.com

To my two beautiful and talented daughters. Annabell & Piper. May you always dream big and settle for nothing but extraordinary. Mommy loves you to the moon and back. Also my lovely nephew, Jaxson. You give hero's a run for their money and you sir, will move mountains one day. Aunty loves you. And last but not least. All the U.S soldiers that fight for this blessed country and to all the women that stand behind them through thick and thin! God Bless.

D. C. Garriott

<u>*Chapter One*</u>

A tall well dressed man, makes his way throughout the rain soaked streets of New York City. He splashes his way to a tall building and swings the door open in haste.

Once inside the building, he squeezes into a crowded elevator, filled with impatient men and women in suits. He shoots the young lady next to him a smile, as she rolls her blonde curls with her finger. She gives a polite nod to him then loses eye contact, she blushes at the floor. He heads to the fourth floor. Stepping out, he leads into a room filled with colorful people awaiting his arrival. He politely says."Hello, My name is Alcott."

Alcott, is a very accomplished Pharmaceutical Salesman, partially because he is well spoken, charming and to say the least, captivating in his older years. Well to be completely honest all his years. Complete, with icy gray, well kept hair and a jaw line that could cut glass. One smile and you are drawn in into a haze of humble, self confidence and determination. The women blush and adore and the men? Well, they want to be him.

Alcott Aldwin, has a reputation for being one of the best salesmen Pfizer has ever had. So the sheepish people that he presents to, are his reserved followers. Just begging to be released out in to the world with his words and possibly, be just as great. Alcott begins to set up a presentation. He is reporting on the use of Abilify for bi-polar disorder. The in and outs of communicating with doctors, to sell them the product. They would need to do all the research possible on the drug

Refuse to Sink

plus, research on the doctor his/her self. He explains. Pharmaceutical salesmen have often been referred to as the Jehovah Witnesses of the sales world. They don't give up. You have a sign out saying the famous: No solicitors, they ignore it. You say, "No Thanks" they ignore it. Persistence, that's how you sell. And lack of humility. You have to have that to get doors slammed in your face all day.

"Some Doctor's will shoo you away." Alcott announces. "And what do we do when this happens?" He questions his audience.

In unison they repeat back to him. "We always go back."
"You all are listening!" He exclaims with a smile. "Never back down. Never Cease. Because these people need what we are selling." he says with his hands in the air. "Its not like we are selling donuts or girl scout cookies. We are selling LIFE IMPROVEMENT!" He shouts in awe of himself.

The young ears hang on his every word as he goes through his power point. He might as well had become a teacher from what he has accomplished over the years. Judging by the magnetic glances of the eager eyes that surround him, he is. He modestly says "Thank You" and his "Have a nice days." Offering some encouraging words to the young salesmen and saleswomen to be.

Feeling very proud of himself. Alcott leaves the room with his head held high, so light on his feet. He is certain that the wind and rain could surely lift him off the ground. He gleefully hails one cab, then the next, never losing the excitement in his voice. He's going home today after being gone for three weeks.

Fantasizing about the smells of home and the smiles on his families faces and the relaxation of his easy chair. Alcott, has been on this speaking tour for what seems like a year. His love ones are back home awaiting his arrival and he misses their faces terribly.

Wiping off the excitement of the day and the rain, he travels down the block to find a cab driver that will give him the pleasure of getting out of the rain. He spots a yellow cab sitting at a stop sign. He races to the curb on the opposite side of the cab, throwing his arms up and down yelling. "Hey buddy! Got room for me?" The cab driver waves him over.

When Alcott locks eyes with old man, he interprets a look of fright and warning. So Alcott looks both ways, to monitor the traffic. He jerks his head to the left. He sees a masked man with a crow bar and before he can react he feels it. His left leg shoots searing pain, like

D. C. Garriott

lighting bolts to his brain, he falls hard to the muddy trash filled curb. He crashes to the ground so fast, he feels his arm crush underneath his weight.

The pain is masked by the car alarm going off in his head. The buzzing and beeping shields him from the beating that is taking place. The sounds are so loud, little white blinks fill his eyelids its all he can do to squint his eyes and unclench his ears. Water splashes his face smelling of copper and rust. The frightened by standers rush off, leaving Alcott helpless. The cabby grabs his phone in hast and dials 911, all the while shouting from his car. "Let him go you fools!"

Alcott can feel the rush of blood coming from his temple and the emptiness filling his body. He rests his head helplessly on the pavement and waits. As they fish through his belongings and take what they want. Including his wallet, his phone most of all, his dignity. As he lay in a puddle choking on his own blood he hears it.
"What are you waiting for? Finish it for gods sake" .
Alcott forces out. "No.. please NO."

The sound of the piano begins to play throughout his battered subconscious then fades out to silence as Alcott draws his last breath.

And in an instant Alcott is gone forever, via gun shot to the heart.

~*~

Refuse to Sink

D. C. Garriott

1900 Blueberry Lane, Kittery ME

"My hometown holds more beauty than any the world has to offer."

Kittery, is situated between the Atlantic Ocean and the Piscataqua River, just north of the New Hampshire border. Settled in 1632, by the British, it is Maine's oldest settlement. Many of the state's ancient homes are still located here. My families Folk Victorian, sits quietly on the side of an old country road. The navy blue shutters are painted with the shaded outline of trees, nestled within the popular Lewis Farm Conservation. A white porch swing sways in the breeze and the smell of pollen is interrupted by my mothers fresh baked strudels, that she is all to famous for.

As a child I can remember three things about my mother. The way her hands smelled of cherry when she would take my temperature or wipe the tears from my face after a biking accident. How she always walked so softly. She was like a breeze. You never heard her walking across the 100 year old solid wood floors that always seemed to creak, if anyone heavier than 80 pounds walked on them. And those strudels. The smell of the baked sugar and creamy fruit filling, always commanded my attention. They made sure that will power stood no chance against them. I remember three things about my father. He was a crack up, his laughter captivating. But he was always gone.

She has been in there for days making pie after pie. I honestly think she is losing her mind. Ever since the news came from New York, that my father had been killed on 5th Avenue. She hums. She has been listening to the same jazz song over and over again. I don't even think it has words. Just the piano, she loved music such as this. In all my life I have heard her actually play music with lyrics maybe once. Pianists are a dime a dozen in Maine.

There are festivals, in Cape Breton probably twenty times a year. They all show off what the ocean breezes and beautiful landscapes have given them. Most of them, still live with their mothers and have very little life aspirations. Yet, my mother goes every year and buys the CD's. And in turn falls in love with these unknown artist.

Refuse to Sink

I guess everyone has their own taste, she just likes the sound a piano makes. I can respect that. It must be a song she and my father shared. He was also enchanted by the white keys. The piano narrates my dreams, the smooth ivory keys are a part of me, as it is part of my mother and my father. They made sure of that. My talent on the musical instrument is fairly good. I feel like I should play for her now, more often. My father was a distinguished pianist though he never took one lesson. It seemed like he was good at a lot of things that he was never taught or trained to do. His hands just found the right keys at the right time, his talent for everything else I guess was the same. Right keys, right time.

He was a great father and she a great mother. My family had always been close. Very close, considering the fact that my father was in New York four times a year and worked in Caribou half the year, then New Brunswick the other half. So he was more of a ghost in the house, than an actual father figure. Yet I still respected my father. As if he were there everyday, teaching me how to fish and catch bees. As I have done for my little brother all these years, without his help.

I took my father's place for years. I never wanted his absence to affect my little brother, the way it affected me. It started when my little brother Chance, turned three. I built him his first fort. I constructed it from old tree bark and leaves, which he had gotten poison ivy from and attacked by a hornet defending his nest. I was banned from building him anything ever again. But that never stopped me from helping him up on his bike when he had fallen and scraped his knee and teaching him the right way to eat a push up Popsicle. Chance never seemed to get the "push up" part and always ending up with his face smashed down into it, wiggling his tongue around to reach the bottom. I would just shake my head and push the little straw upward towards his open mouth.

He used to love to hide in the back yard, that stretched for miles through the towering evergreens. I would count long enough for him to get out of sight, then sniff him out like a trained German Sheppard. Our bond was strong, because it needed to be. We had each other, then we embraced our charismatic father when he did appear.

I still remember the last trip my father made home.

D. C. Garriott

Chapter Two

The curtains wisp rapidly through the open bay window. I sat atop a cushioned bench, tucked into a ceiling high bay window, in the ample living room. Glancing every so often at the leaves falling gracefully from the trees, quietly writing in my journal. Its not weird for a guy to write in a Journal. Don't you roll your eyes in judgment of me. Anyways moving on.

It was fall, the air was crisp, with delicate chill. I become distracted when I hear the screen door swing open and his voice fills the air. My father was always so excited to see us, that I wondered how he could ever live without us while he was away. My father takes a look around long enough to notice that none of the family photos had been changed around. Nor the countless porcelain figures been harmed while he was away.

My little brother liked to throw things and break things like all children do and twice before the sentiments my father adored fell victim. So I'm pretty sure he fears the demise of his cherished figurines every time he walks through that big crystal door. My father always hated when my mother would rearrange things, because it felt less like home when she did. He has said, he likes to imagine what life was like when he was a away and picture where we are, and what we are doing. He always used to say. "I can't reminisce when you move things every second Thursday Wynna." I believe my mother has a small case of undiagnosed O.C.D. I am sure it killed her not to scoot the couch around and reposition the coffee table, but she heeded to his wishes.

The white mantel stretches high on the pale sage walls with all its glory and still dons his most prize possessions. Unharmed and safe. He sighs in relief that the gifts he had given my mother, were still there for

Refuse to Sink

her viewing pleasure. Since he knows how much she misses him while he is away. I assume this makes him feel better about his absence.

Bellowing down the spiral staircase,shoots(literally, shooting finger guns) is my younger brother Chance. He was given this name because the doctors told my mother she had no *chance* of another child after I was born. Apparently, I ruined her. My birth took place in the upstairs bathroom. Given the fact that my arrival was a bit sooner than my parents had planned, by thirty days. My father was away at a seminar for a new anti-convulsion drug, so my mother was forced to go it alone. By the time the ambulance showed up, she had her baby cuddled up on her chest and she lay in a pool of blood. She always jokes, "Anchor waits for NO one."

I grin at the sight of Chance. He jumps, well leaps into my fathers arms, like he had been gone a year. Which he was only in fact gone two weeks, this time. Chance never seemed to be angry or sad while he was away, just pure anticipation for his return. He would constantly say. "My daddy will be home soon enough and then you will get it, Anchor!" I knew what ever I did to anger him into the empty threat,would be forgotten by the end of the day. And most certainly before he returned. I like to think Chance developed an Army brat mentality. You know they are away, you also know they will return and you just get used to it. I never developed this state of mind. I always missed him, it wasn't sadness it border lined between envy and self pity. I respected him. Chance glorified him and my mother adored him.

My Father being the gift giver of the family hands Chance a green bag that reads "Zoo" on it. He opens it, to find a stuffed monkey. Chance takes the monkey and almost immediately, begins to make monkey noises. He throws his arms around my father in excitement, making the hug last then speeds back up the stairs to reunite the monkey with the rest of his toys.

My mother Wynna, (I'm sure my grandmother had a sense of humor when naming her as well) Glides down the hallway, wiping the dish water off her hands onto a apple embroidered apron she is wearing. She tucks her short brown hair behind her ear. She looks up at him with a slight smile, as if she is embarrassed by him catching her like this. Being married for 20 years now. I don't see how that's possible. Nevertheless, it always seemed like they were more in love with each other when they reunited this way. My father hands his wife a bag that reads, "New York City" she unwraps a porcelain lady liberty and reaches up to embrace him in thankfulness. When he picks her up off her feet and squeezes her so hard I am convinced her fragile figure, might break. They linger there awhile, as I walk towards my father. He glances at me and smiles. My father releases my mother and she goes to the mantel, to places the figure next to all the other figurines, that are so important to the two of them. I join my father in the large entrance, which was probably the most inviting room in the house. It would run straight into the spiraling staircase lined with family pictures of us at the ports, chasing puffins and lounging on the beaches of South Maine. He says to me. "Hello Anchor, how's work?" I reply. "Its work, and it doesn't keep me near busy enough"

This is a private attack on my father. He knows I don't care for the line of work he is in, that keeps him away from us so long. I work only part time since graduation, at the golf course a town away. Nothing like picking up golf balls all day, to drive a perfectly sane man insane. But it was a job and paid well enough for my vacation of fun before college. Which my dad didn't agree with either. He expected me to go to NYC right away, but something never felt right. I think that feeling would ultimately turn out to be laziness.

"Oh well idle hands my son, Idle hands" he says with a hint of laughter."I have something for you." he exclaims.

Since he hardly ever brings things other than wise words for me, I was curious. He unwraps a globe and hands it to me. I take the globe, shake it up in confusion. "It's the City" he exclaims. I raise an eye brow and look at him. "Its not a corny gift for a man is it?" he laughs awkwardly. "No dad, its just…." I was interrupted by his laughter, which I always thought sounded a little like Santa Clause.

"I got it for you because when I leave for New York, I work in this building." He points to a small building, I can barely make out. "It's the Empire State Building, one day you will have to go with me."

I shake my head and dismiss the comment since he knows. I don't do big city's. There is something about all the clamor and bustle of big cities. I don't even like going to the ports. Having to weave through tourist and loud music. My soul is stuck in the silence of Kittery. I am easy going and that's how I like my surroundings.

"Well until then son, you can look at this and know where I am."

Refuse to Sink

He grabs my shoulder and gives the snow globe a shake close to his over sized smile. "I love you Anchor, and miss you and my other Aldwin's!" He exclaims, while he sets the rest of his traveler supplies down for my mothers inspection and heads off to the kitchen, probably for some of that strudel. My mother had us all hooked on them like crack. Yep, just like crack.

That was the last time I saw my father. The last days he spent in the house, he worked so hard for. The last time he sat in the living room, in that plush armchair he loved so much and searched for the remote he was always losing in the cushions. The bitter end to his stories of the crowds and city cafes. The last time I heard the laugh of Santa Clause. The day my brother lost his Santa Clause. It hits me in the face; like a brick.

D. C. Garriott

I stand atop the hill in front of my fathers grave. As the flowers are being tossed and the tears being shed. I see my little brother clutching his little monkey that is tattered and torn, due to him keeping it on him constantly since our father's passing. He has been rubbing it between his fingers in nervousness. Chance is holding my mothers hand so tightly. For the first time in my semi adult life. I want to hold her hand too.

She is gripping her handkerchief. Wiping away more tears than I have ever seen her shed in my whole life. She never had any reason to shed tears such as this. Even though people have died that we knew, her grandmother her father and my fathers, father. Still, these tears are pure and have never been needed before. I look away from her blood shot eyes and look down at the eulogy. I must struggle to read. I catch my breath and brush my hair back out of my eyes and begin.

A limb has fallen from the family tree,
I keep hearing a voice that says "Grieve not for me."
Remember he best times, the laughter, the song.
The good life I lived, thanks to my loved ones.
Continue traditions, no matter how small.
Go on with your life, don't worry about falls. I miss you all dearly, so keep up your chin. Until the day comes when we are together again.

A hush falls over the crowd and I am relieved. The preacher breaks the silence with the reading of scripture and the prayer to end the service. Tears begin to dry among the crowd of mourning friends and family. I guess they would, because they have all but forgotten him by now. But he is still a part of our lives, even in death and will always be.

I lay my head down on the night of my fathers interment, forcing the horrible images that I have seen to the back of my mind. My father laying there asleep, in a maroon casket. He lay upon his white silk eternal bed. The delicate lining, filled with the only earthly possessions he could take with him. My mother placing a statue of Dick Tracy(His favorite detective)beside him. My brother placing his monkey safely beside his father. The tears drip down, staining the satin. Chance gripping the handles. And last. My tear ridden mother pulling him away in hast, as he wails a few last "I love you daddy's."

All the faces of people I've never seen before crowd my sub

Refuse to Sink

conscious, lingering on my eyes lids. I want them to scatter but they stare, like doped up rats trapped in a cage. Their faces scare me as I drift into a world I fear. The concrete stretches for miles into the sky, faces that were worrisome,yet normal begin to morph into disfigured, savage creatures calling out to me in angry voices. I turn to run, my legs become weak, causing me to trip and fall. I taste blood and my head tingles from anxiety. I scramble to my feet, running as fast as I can. The faces are still in front of me. As fast as I run, still I cannot out run them. There is a sensation of blood dripping down the back of my neck. With every heart beat, it pumps harder and faster, dripping to the ground and blanketing my eyes with a red glow. I feel around and touch a gaping hole in the back of my head.

My father brings my sprint to a stop. I run straight into him with all my force. He stands so massive, like a giant building. I look high up and try to come to grips with the fact that, he *is* the Empire State Building. In all my confusion. I fall hard to the ground. As he begins to speak, it feels like I have water filling my ears. I can barley make out the words from the distance. I notice a smile on his face. There are people walking around inside the tiny windows, as if they know nothing of the speaking building. He winks and begins to grow smaller, then releases his form as the building and grips my arms embracing my frame.

I feel his heart beating against mine and hear him whisper. "The Flowers are yet to bloom my son." I stand in confusion. I never usually doubted what my father said, but this just doesn't connect. Since when have I given any thought to flowers? He sees my discomfort, so he releases me and reaches down to pick a dandelion from a crack in the concrete. "Take this gem and treasure it." I shake my head and begin explain to him, its just a weed. He begins to fade away.

Before I know it the glare of morning, forces my body to raise up. My eyes still glazed with bewilderment and burning from the salty tears of yesterday's torment. As I stretch out my hands to the ceiling I feel comfort, as if my father was trying to tell me something and that maybe he will be there. Tucked away in my dreams. So at least he's not gone forever.

D. C. Garriott

<u>Chapter Three</u>

If you have ever lost a parent or lover even heaven forbid, a child. You know what it is like to crawl out of bed and sleep with a broken heart. The feeling in your body, that you don't want to face the day, the week, even the toaster. The sunlight mocks you, the moon befriends you. Your veins burn, your eyes twitch and grow tired looking. You are useless soul, that begs to die. If you can muster through the day, you can rarely get anything accomplished, throughout the faint fog that clouds your mind. It is an understatement to say, "*I am hurt.*" It's more of an emptiness, an aching. And it feels like it is permanent, maybe it is.

You're not battered and bruised on the outside. So when you walk down the street, people smile at you not knowing exactly how broken you are. Offering condolences, that may be half heart-ed and definitely half accepted. If only the scars and suffering were to show like a wounded animal. Then maybe, they would help and not forget so soon, that you are damaged. But then again, what would be the point? When you are like this, you don't want their help anyways.

In the aftermath of my father's passing, my brother and I spent the next few weeks consoling my mother and helping out in every way we could. When she got the news that we were going to lose the house, it was by far the worst day since we laid my father to rest. I can hear my mother yelling at the bank on the other end of the phone. Using words I have never heard her use. I had to cover Chances ears a few times a day. I flirted with the notion to just place noise canceling earphones on his ears until all this blew over. But then they might be on there forever. And that's no way to live. Right?

"What do mean that we don't own it??? How can this be?" she shouts. "You have to be kidding me! I don't even know what refinancing means!" she exclaims

Refuse to Sink

"Huh? Right." she falls silent for a moment. "Okay, okay. I understand, so what do I do?" she calms down and takes the advice. They tell her, she will get a settlement and that she would most likely not get enough to cover the house, maybe not even a house at all. I feel her aggravation, like an em path. She is angry at him, sad to not have him and confused as to his motives for refinancing the house, they have owned for years. I touch her shoulder, to try to absorb a small part of her discomfort. When I know, not a soul in the world could relieve the pressure of the world crashing down on her.

She needs to plan on figuring out where to move and when to sell. My mother is no ordinary mother. She always worked whether she worked at a restaurant or a hospital, doing night janitor work. She worked, cooked, cleaned and raised us boys. She is currently a certified nursing assistant at the local nursing home. Since she has no college degree, she is limited but never let it stop her from making money for the family. Even though my father made plenty for us, she always wanted her own and I respected her for that.

The remaining weeks consist of my mother filling out countless forms, packing up my fathers stuff, donating and selling. Strangers begin to flood the house, potential buyers, realtors and family. Some go through our stuff, some came bearing gifts and food. And some just came to see how we were. I guess to check a "Good Deed" off their list of things to do. Before we know it, the house is sold. It was a beautiful house. Buyers had been asking about it for years. Its not surprising it sold so fast. In today's economy, your lucky to sell within a year. We sold in thirty one days.

The big red sign donning the word **SOLD** hangs on the wooden post in the front yard swaying in the breeze. Mocking us as we set and eat our last and final dinner, in the house I have called home since birth.

As we force down the over cooked meat. I think it was supposed to be beef stew, that went terribly wrong. My mother never made anything that tasted bad. I watch her while she eats. I notice that her eyes are glazed over and she is staring blankly into her bowl. She glances up at me when she feels my stare. I smile softly. "Its good mah…." with pity.

Chance picks around at the so called dinner and says. "I don't even know what this is." I shoot him a look,eyebrows down. Chance sticks his tongue out at me and continues to pluck out the pieces he is familiar with.

D. C. Garriott

"Eat it or starve." my mother snaps back at him. She starts to hum. I recognize the tune. Its my parents wedding song. *To Make You Feel My Love.* She hums and we all grow quiet, listening in deep silence. Reflecting on our lives in soft remembrance of our father. The fourth chair sets eerily empty.

A tear drips down my young brothers face, he wipes it away. He stands up and shoves the bowl of gruel away, turns around and walks to the other side of the small cafe table yanking the chair away in a fit of fury. The chair flies into a mound of boxes ironically labeled Alcott. He stomps off through the piles of boxes up to where his room used to be. "I'll go" I stand. "Sit down Anchor." She says softly. "But.. He's - " I am interrupted. "He's fine. He has to deal with it on his own. Let him be." She wipes a single tear on her apple apron as she gathers the bowls to wash.

The night falls softly over the room. I kiss my mother goodnight. Heading up to Chance's room. I pass what seems like a thousand boxes. Full of our families legacy and my fathers memory. I steady myself on the stairs and plop down. My head in my hands, I sob. I miss my father.

The next morning. I rise up off the last remaining rug that we had to sleep on and stretch. I unsteadily travel to the kitchen, grab the cereal, a bowl and milk and look desperately for a spoon. My eyes still swollen. I have to wipe them a few times, just to glimpse out of them. I hear something in the living room. I shut the drawer with my hip and cart the breakfast back into the half empty room. I see my brother laying across my mother, wiping the hair away from her face. She is glued to the rug in sorrow, weeping and holding on for dear life.

She didn't want to go, she looked like a small child throwing a tantrum. She was so scared, lonely and grief stricken that she couldn't even move. My father has been dead for forty five days, she is finally breaking down. My little brother musters all the strength he has left and is trying to console her saying. "It will be alright Mommy, daddy would want us to move on to be okay. Don't you think mommy?"he waits for an answer.

She says nothing. He breaks down as well. He lays down lightly next to her, with his tiny arm draped over her waist. I am still standing in the hallway, arms filled with food, looking like the asshole that was hungry at this hugely important moment. I set my food down and go to help my mother up. She comes willingly, she wipes her eyes on her

Refuse to Sink

nightgown and says. "Chance stop crying you are right, he would. Better get a move on things we need to be there by nightfall"

"I'll drive mom, you just grab that cereal I am starving. And Chance make sure you go to the bathroom. I am not stopping every five minutes!" I say sternly.

My mother looks at me through her embarrassment, like she wants to say something. But she just looks away, continuing to pack. I know what she's thinking. I sound just like my father. He was always so impatient on car trips. Even though we rarely took them.

One trip I remember, we went to Prine Edward Island in the fall. I couldn't swim in the ocean, because it was negative something degrees. I recall throwing a fit, asking why they would bring a child to the ocean and not let them get wet. It was cruel and even now I still don't get it.

"Maine in Autumn, is something to remember for a lifetime. It's a symphony of natural beauty" my mother used to say.

She loved where she lived. It was a choice, she wasn't born in this state. Nether was my father. My mother was born in Alabama, my father in Illinois. My mother used to tell me as a child, she used to dream of the ocean and lighthouses, she had seen in the magazines and school books. She has said before,that her dreams lead her here. She did not grow up in a what *normal* folks would call a loving home. When she was seven her mother lost her husband, in some war I could never recall.

Resulting in my grandmother left to raise 4 children alone. See back then they did not have 300,000 dollar payouts, if your spouse is killed in combat. Yes, that is how much a family gets these days for losing there whole world. Doesn't seem like enough does it? My grandmother was angry at her children. I guess because she was overwhelmed, or maybe she just took her sadness out on them. Never the less, it was a hostile environment.

I have seen my grandmother three times and received one gift from her, in my whole nineteen years. I hear my mother speak to her on the phone, it is always so mechanical not one ounce of softness. I think

D. C. Garriott

my father loved her more, because she lacked it from her mother.
On any account. She deserved the extra love and what spilled over she gave to us children as a "Just in case you didn't know how much you are loved." offering.

After graduating high school, she used all the money she had saved and received as gifts from family. My mother set out to find the place she calls home now. She had a plan in her head, and all be damned if she didn't accomplish all the dreams she set out for herself. She met my father, while working at a gas station on the outskirts of Kittery. He had stopped in on the way back to Illinois. She has said, it was love at first sight. (Which I don't believe in) My father would concur. He claimed, it was love at first word. He would describe it as the most desirable word, ever spoken in the English language. He fell in love when she said. "Welcome"

I always used to inquire about this story when I was younger, when he would describe their first meeting, my father would always say. "She said WELCOME TO MIDWAY!" he explained he only heard "*Welcome*" And that was it, he was gone. Lost to her forever. I always giggled and wondered if that really could happen? I loved the story anyway. Even if they were full of shit.

They settled right in the town they met, for remembrance sake I suppose. Still it is a wonderful place and a great environment to grow up in. Small town love I suppose. If you have ever lived in a small po - doke town, you know exactly what I speak of. Everybody knows your name and speaks kindly of you, even if you didn't deserve it. When I was in high school, my mother would say that I brought a bit of smut to her beautiful town. This I guess was in reference to my casual encounters with the cheer leading team and the hearts I undeniably left broken, on that serene Victorian porch. I didn't do any of it on purpose. I was a lustful teenager, occupying my boredom with the "Symphony of the trees" and concentrated on the "Symphony of the first kiss." Which I had many of. I would consider myself charming, capricious, even a little whimsical. None which ever seemed to amuse my mother, who was constantly defending my childhood.

My mother used to always call me a hippie. I never knew what that meant until history class. I saw myself in the black and white pictures. My hair was really long at one time. I never thought that I had sub consciously based it on the 60's. But maybe my natural, rebel insides

Refuse to Sink

spilled out on my hair. I have just recently cut it, to my mothers pleasure. But I don't like to comb it, so she remains semi- displeased.

I look just like my father. I have his stick thin legs and his broad shoulders, his bright aqua blue eyes, that I think are a huge help with the ladies. *Thanks Dad.* But since he was gray headed for most of my life. I would have to look back and find out through pictures and videos, that he gave his blonde hair to my little brother and I received my mix of sienna and blonde, from my mother. My mother's hair color has changed over the years, since she refuses to look old.

I don't suppose she could ever look old. She has zero wrinkles and no physical ailments. I think she might be a vampire. I once thought she was a Christmas elf, but then I realized she was sleeping with Santa. And that didn't make sense. Maybe she once was never-aging, but I have a feeling with the resent turn of events, the years may begin to catch up.

D. C. Garriott

Chapter Four

The car is heavily loaded down, with the only parts of our lives that weren't for sale or just weren't considered important to the buyers. I made sure that I kept two of my fathers business suits. Also a couple of his sweaters that I loved. Not cool for a young man to wear his fathers clothes? Dead or alive? But I have never been one to care about fads, nor have I ever worried what others thought. The car ride is long and tiring, after about two hundred miles. I pull into a gas station and my mother tells me to switch her positions. After a huge iced honey bun and chocolate milk, my eyes grow heavy. I slide into the passenger seat lay my head against the window, with my jacket as a pillow. I drift off to sleep.

The city is sparkling, the trees are green. I walk along a glowing copper path, with my father. He shouts at me for picking flowers, that apparently are not supposed to be bothered. If I had a dollar for every time he yelled at me over something so small. I'd be rich. He had the misfortune of miss picking battles with me. Of course I stop enjoying the flowers, because the enforcements would have just not been worth it. I grab my fathers hand. It is so heavy like steel, mine so small as it sets inside. If he were to clinch his fist, my hand would surely be crushed. I am confused as to why am I holding my fathers hand? I never did that. In my eighteen years I think the only time I held his hand, was when I needed to cross the street in kindergarten.

I hold on tight and look up at him, like a child. He is smiling, we are almost skipping. He skips so fast; I cant keep up. I yell. "Slow down Daddy! I am falling behind" he begins to pull me down. I am being dragged. The rocks beneath me cut my legs and my shoes fly off. "Keep up son we've got places to be, pull yourself up" he yells. I wonder why cant I catch my bearings? He begins to let go. I hold on tighter; I'm losing grip and its gone.

Refuse to Sink

His hand is gone. He continues to skip, until he is in a full on sprint. I watch him until he is out of sight. He seems to have ran into a pool of bright lights, splashing through the sparkles of light that flood the ground. It hurts my eyes to look in that direction. So I turn away, the air turns to complete darkness and I can hear my mother calling me, from somewhere outside my dark bubble.

"Anchor? Hello? Boy? Wake Up!" she shouts. I feel a slap to my forehead and I exit the darkness, returning to the passenger seat of the car. My head throbs and my little brother giggles from the backseat.
"What were you dreaming about Anchor? You were moving all around. You must have been tired." She sounds aggravated. "You know you don't need to be driving when you are that tired! You didn't last a minute over there and you were out! You know soon you will be out of the house, living on your own. And now I have to worry about your sheer lack of self control!" shaking her finger in my face.
Really? Jesus, Whatever! Is what I wanted to say. But this is all that came out.
"I know I'm sorry." with a hint of guilt. She was just taking out a little misaddressed anger. So I let her have it. She has enough going on without my mouth making it worse.

As we pass attractions along the way, my brother shouts in pleasure. We stop at a small Diner, for a bite to eat. Chance acts like its the first meal he has eaten in days. Which I'm sure is accurate, since he has been picking at his food for quite sometime. My mother describes the town we are moving to, as modest and unique. She illustrates a memory she and my father had on vacation here, before we were born and she cleverly makes it sound delicious. Not the town, but life before my brother and I. Her eyes twinkle as she remembers the trip, and I wonder if she has a chance of love again, without the looming memory of my father.

"Your father begged me for boys. And he use to chant "Go team Go!" to my full belly, in hopes for a star player. She explains.
I'm sure he was disappointed with my lack of athleticism. He tried to get me to play tee ball, basketball and football. But I always found sports to be tiresome and at the very least boring as hell. My only competition in high school, were the boys he wanted so desperately for me to be. I smile, as I recall the day I didn't get picked for the basketball team. He said to me.

D. C. Garriott

"Well boy, at least you got that cheerleaders number." He got me. He knew that's the only reason I was there in the first place. After that debacle he just shined in my inappropriate glory. Nicknaming me "Anchor, the King of Smut" Or "Smutty Bagersfield" that one was just weird. My brother was a little better at sports than I. He played soccer for our home team and even scored some leading points, in a couple of games. Which my father was only there to see once or twice. He was absent far more often, since Chance was born. I don't think my father was disappointed in me. Just "more pleased" with Chance. As we all were. I look to the backseat at my brother setting up straight; reading his comic. He glances at me and rolls his eyes, as if he was deriding my memory.

Chance is a strong, well mannered, charming little boy. I couldn't blame anyone for falling in love with him. My flow of anamnesis is interrupted by my mothers shrieking. "We're here boys, look alive!" she says with excitement.

The car pulls onto a gravel driveway, the car bumping and throwing dirt behind it. This is first I have seen of life in my mother for weeks. So when I look at the rugged, small house with tattered curtains hanging in the windows. I force a smile that I hope; she cant see right through. I get the feeling that pirates may have lived here before us and left it in complete disarray, for which they alone are known for.

The dark, lifeless, wood, looks like it has been rotting for years. The foundation is in serious trouble, it's cracked and tattered. And if I'm not mistaken, is spray painted gray? I don't know much about houses, but I do know this is a poor excuse for one. The other houses are in just as bad of shape. One sits to the left and one to the right. One just as awful as the other. The sun is setting. I see a glow around the house I didn't notice before, probably because I was to busy judging the poor. It's beautiful and makes the house look almost livable. I wonder if its my dad shining down on the dilapidation saying. "Its gonna be okay son. This will work for now."

I take it as a sign of grand intervention and quit with the automatic judgment and decide to give it a chance. Watching my mothers actions. I mimic her excitement when my brother walks near, trying to ease the pain of this change. I turn sour as soon as he is out of sight. I help my mother unpack the boxes from the small U-Haul, we pulled behind our station wagon for six hundred miles.

Refuse to Sink

A lot of boxes have spilled out and pictures broken. This makes my job harder and aggravates me to no end. My mother approaches and realizes the look on my face is all too unpleasant. She exclaims although tired.

"Turn that frown upside down, Charlie Brown!" Really? She is so annoying right now. My mother is known for her corny one liners. But this is just ridiculous. I shoot her a grin, even though I am surely wishing that she would burst into flames.

Around the car; I hear a giggle. It couldn't possibly be my torn and misplaced, little brothers laugh. Which I haven't heard in weeks. Yet I agree to myself that in fact, my bothers laugh could pass as a girls. This brings a smile to my face. I am confronted by a small girl that seems foreign tanned with ebony black hair that draped across her back, like satin. She is already too pretty for her age, which would have to equal to my brothers, give or take a year. She looks up at me with big, bright brown eyes that the light catches ever so softly. She has a look on her face that confirms, she dislikes me immediately.

"Hello…" says the little Pocahontas. I reply with a smile. "Hello Pretty." The little girl blushes, and wipes the disgust from her face as quickly as she put it on. With a flip of her long black hair she questions." I'm Aria. A-r-i-a. I don't see any animals?"

"Nope, my mother is allergic to pets. And my name is, Anchor. A-n-c…." she interrupts my spelling game.

"I know how to spell Anchor. What? Is she allergic to happiness as well!" she exclaims with the disgust reappearing. I think to myself. If she only knew.

"No I don't think so, but I'm real busy so if you don't mind. My little brother is inside. I believe he is your age if you would like to meet him" I note. She agrees and heads inside. The two children meet and immediately hit it off, as all children do. They begin to discuss the rules of hide and seek then are gone from sight. My mother and I finish unloading the little trunk of precious cargo, that holds the key to our past. *So pirate like.* I think, as we head into the abandoned ship for the night. I silently laugh; and yell for Chance to join us. Sending his newly found friend back to the dim lit home, she previously hailed from. I watch as she walks home. And see a woman open the door and usher her in. Its probably her mother, inquiring about the Raiders Of the Lost Ark. She hopefully, will explain we are indeed normal people, with no pirate tendencies.

D. C. Garriott

Dinner is set, it includes left over PB&J sandwiches and chips, left over from the car trip. My mother pours the kool aide from the canister, into paper cups. The three of us set in a semi circle, around a box labeled Living room.

We talk about the road trip. What time I am to rise in order to make sure Chance is at the bus stop on time. My mother's job interview is tomorrow. My mother always planned ahead, she already had Chance in a school and for her, a new job. (hopefully) And for me, a well thought out map of the new town, to assist in my job search. She was many things to me. She is my mother, my friend, my drill sergeant and my tender guide. As I sit and look at her. I cant imagine a woman ever taking her place in my heart.

Morning comes all to fast. That rearing, uncomfortable feeling reappears yet again; as it does every morning. You wake up hoping when you open your eyes, that your life hasn't changed. Then you realize, it is still hell on earth. Your heart shatters over and over again. My first thought was: *I'm not the only person in this room having that same feeling.* One big sigh later. I raise up off my uncomfortable mat and off the contaminated living room floor. I think to myself. *Bed. I wanna go back to bed. Not the floor.* I hesitantly rise up with a limp, pretty sure I aged fifty years over night. My mother is laying there still, which is shocking, she is usually up well before us making something; anything in the kitchen. I look at her sleeping, saddened for a while. I feel regret for her awaking moment, and Chance's. I don't want to disturb their sleep. Because I know they are both somewhere peaceful, with dad. I realize the time my mother had before this, was for her and her baking and she will no longer get to do that. She must work forty hours a week to hold on to a less than poverty stricken life for her children. I immediately feel anger. This is not her fault, she doesn't deserve this. I push the animosity aside, deciding this is truthfully no ones fault. Holding on to anger is a sickness, and I intend to be well… One day.

I shake my brother awake. He fights the daylight but arises to face the new day and new school. I cant imagine what it must be like for him. He is entering a new school with only months left till summer, and he has exactly no people skills. Chance is shy, awkward and now since he is pirate offspring, he will be dubbed as weird. Which is fitting for him because he is weird. With stringy blonde hair that never cuts straight and a nose he inherited from my grandpa, that is straight and lacking of

Refuse to Sink

nostril. He is a bit wormy, with a slight scar above his left eye(somewhat pirate like) that he got snow boarding in the park. It was a wicked wreck, that I enjoyed fully. He is just like me when I was a little boy, no need for approval. Always steady in who he is. At such a young age, it must be genetics. Born in to a bloodline, that refuses to let you give a shit about what other people thought was normal or right. *Thanks Dad.*

Also my grandfather, he deserves a little credit for three generations of hell raisers. He fought in World War II, and was deployed to Poland. He survived some of the worst events in American history. And for that, he is a bad-ass. Or at least I thought he was. I looked up to him. When he passed away, they laid a big American Flag across his casket. That was my first memory of tears falling from my eyes.

Chance doesn't fight me on what to eat for breakfast, as if he had a choice in the matter. All that was un packed was a pair of jeans, a t-shirt that read "Redwings" across the front, also two mismatched socks. We ate our brown sugar Pop Tarts cold, in the tiny undecorated kitchen that was completely different from the kitchen I grew up in. I am sure you could have fit one hundred people in there with comfort. I remember my father would have business dinners for clients or students. The lights would dim and they "The Grown Ups" would sit around with wine glasses and cigars. I always wondered what was so funny or so important that their faces would cringe up like they saw a snake. I miss ease dropping. I miss my house. I miss my kitchen. I miss my father. Another deep sigh (This time from both of us) As we head out the ratty door to the bus stop.

While walking up the gravel road. I spoke to Chance about the proper way to address new friends and to try and keep his humor in check. It always came off dry and a bit edgy in tone. I had been the one and only person he would tell a joke to. Ever. I assured him that they were bad. And he should never tell a knock knock joke ever again. He hesitantly agrees. He just didn't have it, the funny bone I acquired from my father and grandfather. A smooth kind of way that I told the joke. That made them flow nicely and have you laughing your pants off, before I even hit the punch line. I take pride in my humor, even though I have heard it referenced to as rude and semi aggressive at times. I take that as a compliment. I continue to lecture him, when I am interrupted by the familiar wailing of the little girl behind the car, one moon ago.

"Hello there Neighbor friends!" she shouts.

D. C. Garriott

I had just wiped the remaining sleep from my eyes and my head begins to pound. Yet she persist. Great.

"Hey! Chance… And Anchor." she pronounces my name in disgust. What is with this kid! Why me? Why does she deter me so? I think its because she has fallen in love with my awesomeness and is devastated to find that; I am out of her age group of love and hates me for all the reasons that little ladies do, that cant have the sweet kiss of unattainable Anchor.

I have experienced this type of behavior before in my younger days. The punch to the back in elementary school, the swat to the shoulder in middle school. I get it. It's the *Tag your It* , kind of love. Isn't that the best kind of love? The kind that wakes you up in the morning with a smile. The excited feeling you would get, when that person came through the classroom doors. And how the day would drag on and on if your crush would happen come down with the flu or chicken pox. I wink at her as she flourishes in the morning light. So pure. And unharmed by fate. Spunky, blissfully happy. I envy her. Silly kid. My thoughts are disturbed by a cordial voice from afar. Across the way I see her. I wipe my eyes again to get a better view.

Refuse to Sink

D. C. Garriott

Chapter Five

It was like a star had fallen from the sky.

Instantly; I remember the story my father had told me all those years ago, about becoming deaf at the sheer sight of someone. She floats toward my brother and I. With such ease and grace. Her white skirt blowing in the morning breeze. I fully expected her to be a ghost and float right pass me. Her hand to her lips, she makes a shushing sound that sounded like the ocean, or did I hear birds chirping? Were there real birds circling around my head? I was knocked almost unconscious, by her beauty. The wind forcing her hair to wisp back and forth across her back. Sending the smell of orchids and cupcakes bursting like fireworks through the air. Her radiant skin the color of dark Arabian sand, yet still lighter than the younger sister. She approaches Chance and I. I can feel the breath being sucked from my lungs, as she begins to speak.

"Hi, My name is Grace Anne Keats. And yours would be?"
I am numb. I don't hear her. I hear Jerry McGuire in my head saying, "You had me at hello" and my inner most person, telling me to snap the hell out of it! Its all I can do to focus. Her eyes. I watch them, as the early sun hits them ever so perfectly, they fade from green to blue then back to green. She holds out her hand to shake mine. I don't move. I'm Frozen. In complete shame of myself.
"Grace. How fitting" I mumble to myself lips half moving. As if it was God himself who named her. I panic. She looks surprised and let down at the level of disrespect I have shown her. She begins to pull her hand away, then places it back to her side. Her face glowing in confusion.
You know; I might as well have been Helen Keller at this moment. Thank God for my younger, less infatuated brother who gladly introduces himself and his mute older brother.

"Hi, my name is Chance. Like fat Chance." he laughs and quickly glances in my direction. She giggles, as if he were really funny? Huh, imagine that! Well at least he can speak in her presence and for that I give

Refuse to Sink

him some credit. Even so. I shoot him a look of please do not do that at school. He gets it and continues.

"And this manly, man is....." the young girl cuts him off. "His name is Anchor. I know its weird. But he is very nice despite his weirdness." she laughs and begins to talk with Chance about something involving shovels.

"Anchor? Very nice. Your mom has a sense of humor?" she laughs. It was exhilarating to hear a real laugh.

Now this may come as a shock, but this is not the first time someone is astounded or humored by my name. When I was in grade school I was constantly teased, until I was mentally numb to any naysayer's. They weren't even clever. My mother, takes full credit for my name. And my slow decent into infinite school yard suicide. "You weighed me down like an Anchor." she would tease. "It really felt like I had one in my belly, carrying you for eight and a half months." I guess I was a heavy baby but to name me after my heaviness, was just cruel.

She is speaking to you Anchor, snap out of it! No time to reminisce! My senses go crazy, warm, fuzzy intoxication. My feet come partially unglued from the pavement, my mouth starts to move miraculously, before I could stop myself I bellow, "We are not pirates!" I close my eyes, praying I didn't say that.

"I. I mean, that's not what Anchor stands for!" I shudder awaiting her response. "Ha!" Chance is clearly entertained. The remaining minutes after my dishonorable mention of the pirates, are filled with coy questions involving our move to her part of town. Also, some less interesting stories from her bird like younger sister. Who just seems to be annoying me, with all of her nonsense. I want to put my hand over her mouth and ask Grace so many questions. Yet, she continues to talk about bugs and a science project due, sucking up all my time for questions, that I desperately needed to ask.

The bus pulls up promptly, the familiar hydraulic doors open wide and they all pile in. Chance waves from the window. I gesture back to him. Placing my index finger over my lips, a warning to him about his previous "Good Humor." Grace Anne turns to me, tossing her backpack around her shoulder. "Well it was nice to meet you, Anchor" she snickers mocking me of course, as she bounces onto the bus. She glances out the window at the fool, standing in the same place I was; the very moment she came draping across the driveway. She smiles and waves a half wave.

28

D. C. Garriott

Almost like the way a beauty queen waves. It was very posh, very grown up. I on the other hand, felt like I should have gotten on the bus with Chance, rode to 6 grade with him and maybe learn a thing or too.

This has never happened to me. I am a charming, off the collar type of guy. I am not the type to feel faint or uncomfortable around a woman. I slay them damn it! I am the Alpha! I become angry at my sub conscience, for being so brash. *You wouldn't want to be like that forever Anchor. Maybe its time I got swept off my feet.*

I replay the conversation(or lack there of) a couple times, before I move towards the house. I wonder what grade she could be in? She could already pass for eighteen. So she couldn't be any younger than sixteen, it would break my heart to hear this news.

This wasn't the first time I have fallen for a younger girl. I once dated a freshman, while I was a senior. I found that my infatuation was not with her, but purely with summertime and by the fall. I had given her up. Something about the sea breeze and tanning lotion, that lowers your bodies sense of age.

She was sixteen and I eighteen. It was not a good fit by any means. But we did fit. If you know what I mean. But after the initial appreciation. I knew, she was a summer girl. A summer girl, is someone you meet mostly at the beach, by a lemonade stand; or late night party on a warm Saturday night. They are never meant to be a long term sweetheart. Yet they fill the shoes as a romantic companion, in the months where you find yourself lonely. When you are without the constant flow of girls in the school year. Jessica(my summer girl) even her name screamed summer time. Jess, had fallen to deep in devotion over the summer. So when I let her go, she begged and pleaded with me. Talking about soul mates and our first child. Nonsense really. I remember shaking my head at her saying. "Jess, you were just a girl at the right place at the right time. It could have been anyone, but you have a nice ass. So I am thankful for that." I later found out that I had stolen her virginity and "ruined" her life. Great.

But when you are a young boy with hormones and a wandering eye, hearts tend to get broken. The world still turns. I guess that's the naive talk of a heart, that has never been crushed. I will be right here when Chance gets off that bus. With any luck, she will speak to me again. I can find out her age, then I will know what I am in for. *Please don't be sixteen, please don't be sixteen.* Now its time to get things done. Focus. I walk

Refuse to Sink

back in the house, to find my mother wiping off counters and fixing her makeup in a broken mirror (a casualty of the trip) almost pirate like. But I digress. She shoots me a look. "I saw the pretty girl you were talking to." She glares at me with a mix of disappointment and anxiety. "Don't you go hurting that sweet girl, Smutty!"

"Well, I wasn't so much talking to her. More like tripping over my lips, she is pretty though huh?" I question her. "Yes. Yes she is Anch. Just don't make her cry boy!" she says with an undertone of laughter.

I wanted to tell her that I believe her and dad now. That I have fallen head over heels in love with a stranger, that their story has come to life right in front of my face. But I didn't think that this was the time to mention dad. She hugs my neck. "Good Luck today son." then heads out the door, letting the screen door slam behind her.

I shower and shave listening to the music on my laptop, dancing to Bob Marley's "Three little Things." Have I completely turned into a swashbuckler? Shaking my head to relieve the water, slinging it across the room and down my naked back. I shiver, turning it to something more current. Something has changed in me.

I don't want to sweep this girl off her feet and tell her lie after lie to make her fall in love with me, lay her then leave her. I want to hold her and breathe her, make her part of me. This is impossible. An impossible turn of events. Even in the aftermath of my father's death. I believe I am indeed, in God's favor.

Heading into town, I hear birds chirping and smell pie. I wish I knew who was making it. I would stop by and ask for a piece, like a homeless traveler. If I didn't have on my new suit. I would. My mother is going to buy me a truck she saw in a newspaper, soon. I suppose till then I will be walking. My mind wonders *Would Grace join me in my "new" truck? Could I get that girl to run away with me?* I begin to blush. I don't blush.

Breaking a sweat I try to focus on something, other than the way her hair shines and lays so softly upon her shoulders. The way her laugh sounds like a cherub.

I contemplate what a cherub would sound like and I'm sure, that would be it. Walking is not all that bad. Maine is always cool it seems, an everlasting brisk breeze combing my brow. The neighborhood I live in sets directly behind an old train station. I walk along the abandoned tracks, until I find myself strolling along main street. The buildings are high and mashed together. The current vista seems largely unchanged,

D. C. Garriott

from that of 1628. There's a lot of people walking along the narrow street. It is nice, it is a nice place to live. Breathing in, feeling relaxed the sun gracing my forehead. Its so similar to my hometown, that I almost feel comfortable. The trees line the street the same way. The sun shines on the sides of the buildings just as it did in Kittery. But I'm no astrologer and I don't know if we are west, north or south of my town, or if it would do that anyway.

The town is juxtaposed with the cobblestone streets, quaint pubs and antique shops. It is early morning, the town is already buzzing. Everyone seems very nice. I smile and wave at a group of ladies, that seem to have hopped right out of a novel written about hot tea and big red hats. They give me a courtesy wave in return.

Nice, but then again most everyone "seems" nice when you first meet. Its only when you get to know most people ,do they show their true colors. Sad people smile, and happy people gossip. Most people are fake down to their core, most people are liars. I am not a cynical person just insightful, if you will.

This town is a bit of a "tourist attraction" because it is the "Most Northeastern City in the United States." And borders New Brunswick and Quebec. It has a lot of attractions, that would explain this constant flow of human traffic. Like the Nylander Museum. The Historical Society's and a super cool Country club, that I would love to work for. I'll mull that one over. I remember the hatred I developed towards golf while dodging balls flying at my head, in my last job.

Maybe they are tourist? Or this town is just crowded? I wonder if they think I'm a tourist? Which technically; I am one. I don't know exactly why my mother chose this town, of all the towns to choose from. Its beauty? No. Its schools? No. I asked her once why Maine? Why this state? And she simply said with a smile. "Its because it's the only United State, mentioned by Shakespeare."

Now, I don't know if that's true, but she seemed to believe in it fully so I have to go on her word. It couldn't be because Maine is divided into eight distinct tourism regions. With 6,000 lakes, 32,000 miles of rivers, five thousand miles of coast and 17 million acres of forestland. I don't know, it just seems that she could find a better reason than Shakespeare.

There should be a lot of opportunities for one able bodied man to find a low paying, ill fitted job around here. Since that is all I have

Refuse to Sink

obtained, post graduation. As I explained earlier. I didn't go to college right away because I needed a break, from doing whatever it was I was doing in high school. Which is a blur now, but I am pretty sure it was important back then. Music Academy at NYC. That was the path that I strayed from. I just wasn't ready, back then.

I say back then, like it wasn't last summer. But I have been through a lot since then, so I have grown up just a bit. I think. But I get it. I am young, new to town and other than this morning's nonsense. I am very personable and can relate to just about anyone.

I pass by a coffee shop/diner, trying not to drag my feet. Job hunting. I hate it. It's like auditioning and they tell you not to take it personally, but you do. Unless you are a self loather. You know you can do that particular job better than anyone else they choose to hire, and it breaks your spirit just a little, not to get the call back. I reach into my pocket, to check if I brought any cash with me. As my belly begins to growl, I panic. I check my front pockets then the back and nothing. "Crap!" I say aloud. Immediately I pull back my tone, as heads jerk in my direction. That's all I need to do, shed light on all my smut. And then I find five dollars, in my shirt pocket.

On my way into the shop it is buzzing with conversations. I overhear a over exaggerated story about the shrimp liner that wrecked near Canada. The frozen man that turned up on the beach, by the docks a couple days ago. I listen in as I sit at the bar, filling out the countless applications I grabbed on my trip so far. Filling out applications is just grueling. Your name, address and social security number over and over. And the "Your last job part" is REALLY difficult, when you've only played your whole life. Would they accept women chasing and casual marijuana usage? Or the entire summer I spent in Panama my Junior year, where I am sure I died twice from Alcohol poisoning.

I also had a girl that summer. Her name was Kortney, with a K. Interesting enough to draw my attention. I could never forget her. She was from Chicago. She had a mob accent and a huge rack. Her blonde hair cascaded around her tan fruitful body, that embraced the tiny barely there neon green bikini like a glove. She held my hair back, as I vomited and brought me lotion when I burned. I helped myself to her and when we departed in August. I told her. I would always love her. Indeed I would always love her, bosoms. Err.. Nah I am sure they don't want to know these things. I cringe in the reflection of my mistakes. I notice a

D. C. Garriott

group of solid men sitting at a circular table across from where I sit. They all look burly and very strong and making my stature look obsolete. I wonder what they do, and why there is a stench coming from that general area? "Seaports, young fellow. That's where you need to be." I hear from behind me. Well that explains the fish smell and discriminating body build. "Really sir? Are they hiring?" I inquired.

"They are always hiring my brother." Sounding and looking a little to much like Hulk Hogan. I wondered if he was trying to?

"I will, I will go down there Thanks! UM.. Could get a referral name?" I pondered aloud.

"Its Paul Wright, good luck little fella." he walks behind my stool, to the cashier and slaps my back so hard; I believe I lost my last baby tooth. Little fella? I wanted to show him little. But I need that name to get my foot in the door. I gobble my food down and head back out into the sun of the streets for the walk back home, to wait for that bus!

On the short trip home, it always seems shorter when you are heading home, than when reaching the destination. At least I always thought so. Grace Anne enters my mind for a brief moment, then my father. I think of what he would say about her. I would probably hear. "Go get um Boy!" or "How bout that one, boy she's a beauty!"

My last girlfriend he used to call Uma. He swore up and down, she looked exactly like Uma Thurman. I just laughed at him and wondered if he saw something I didn't. I mean she was pretty, in a Hollywood kind of way. She was unusually tan for the part of the U.S we lived in, and wore plenty of excess makeup that really didn't do anything, except cause me wonder what she looked like when she took it all off. Which I never got to see, because her backwards views on life shed a light on her, that I never really cared for. So I left the three month relationship with an uninterested. "Well it was nice to have known yah, but I think we have different plans in life." She politely told me to go "F" myself slamming my bedroom door behind her.

That was the only action I ever got in that room, with her.

Refuse to Sink

★

D. C. Garriott

Chapter Six

Maine is known for its lighthouses. I have had my share of fun in them. I use the line. "Hey you wanna go watch some whales?" Then the girls would think; I was an animal lover. I would intentionally take them to a light house with no whales, ever. When we get bored with no whale action, then we would create our *own* action. Now I am in no way, a womanizer. I love women, and respect them. But I love them, and in that respect. I have to have them.

I am taken from my memories, by the smell of baked sugar and cherry, the same smell from earlier this morning. It is coming from a little house, that sits about five down from mine. I see a little old lady, she has to be over seventy bending down pulling weeds, obviously in pain. I walk over and charmingly ask her if I can assist. She obliges. I reach down and begin to pull the pest below the gravel.

My knee touches the ground and she exclaims. "Your mother would die if you ruin your suit messing around at my house!"
"I will explain the importance to her and she will see the error of my ways and all will be well. I never got your name Miss?"
"It is Mrs. Billings" and I have something for you she points to the house. I follow her, hoping that its a slice of pie. She hands me a dollar bill. "For your generosity." she says with pride. I look down at the bill trying not to sound too cocky, when I say. "I'll trade you this dollar for a slice of that pie?" She nods and I score the pie.

All in all a great day for Anchor Alcott Aldwin. I give her my best weed killing pointers, that's she takes into consideration and I bid her ado. Carrying on my way, to the bus stop. I try not to sweat. I attempt to slow the pace of my heart. I am way too excited to just get a glimpse of her. Grace Anne. Oh what a name! It's the most beautiful name I have ever heard. I try to control my sub conscience, after I've said her name over and over in my head a thousand times.

When I reach my new drive way. I look up and see my mother standing in front of her bedroom window. She is looking up at the sky

Refuse to Sink

and if I'm not mistaken, she is talking to herself? Or someone? As I begin to think she has officially lost her mind. I see the tears rolling down her face with force. She wipes the tears away with short strokes, as if she is trying to isolate the tears to just her eyes, to prevent her face from becoming red. I cross the creaking porch, open the door letting it clamor behind me, so I don't shock her in this state and risk embarrassing her. This pulls her out of her room, still wiping and patting her face; I ask. "How was the interview, did you nail it?? Huh? You did, I know you did!"

"It went well Anch. I am a charmer. Where do you think you get it from?" She says with a hint of a smile. She goes on.
"It pays well enough so you don't have to get a job, you just go ahead and apply for school. You've let it go long enough Anchor. I suggest you get your act together." she scolds. I bow to her "As you wish Mother" I reply with sarcastic tone.
"With that mouth you would make a good lawyer, or a shoe in at clown college." she smiles a real smile.

I tip an imaginary hat in acknowledgment for her wicked burn and carry on out the door. With all her strength I am not blind to the fact, that my mother has her weaknesses. She is a sucker for my little brothers art work. She even tears up at the thought of giving her oldest son to another woman one day. She holds it together better than any mother I know, so when she collapses like this. I try to respect her heart. I change the subject or say something witty to make her smile, sometimes it works sometimes she gets aggravated and yells at me. Ether way, she loses the focus that is bringing her down.

When my father would leave and stay gone for weeks. I used to catch her sitting at his piano, in our living room tapping on the keys with a bottle of wine in one hand and a long stemmed glass in the other. I don't think she ever even poured the wine in the glass. She holds a lot back. Worry and sadness never showed on her face until I believe. We went to bed. Its hard for children to understand "Grown up emotions" Parents have to sacrifice a lot. I know that now. They smile when they are sad and laugh when they want to cry out. To us, they are almost robot like. She was not a robot. She had feelings. I saw them. I would like to think she was happy with my father, her children, the life that she chose. But I will never really know.

I find that I am skipping down the drive way. and Gradually stopping myself, before anyone can see me and question my sexuality. It

D. C. Garriott

is three o'clock on the dot. I wait impatiently at the end of the gravel walk, kicking my feet around in the dirt. I draw a heart in the dirt with an A and G on the inside. I don't really take my mothers offer of college into consideration, at least not right now. I will go to the ports and try my best hand at getting that job. She's going to need me, whether she knows it or not. It feels like hours have passed, which I am sure have only been minutes. I hear the lamentation of the bus a block away, crossing the train tracks. The noise gets closer, causing the nervousness to begin building inside me. The butterflies inside my stomach feel like they are in a fight to the death. I begin to sweat. *I never sweat.* I am charming why does this girl make me over heat? Guess I am about to find out.

The bus pulls in front of me, throwing dirt and rocks on my shoes. Quickly, I stomp out the letters in the muck. I see my brothers face smiling and waving at me. Aria, the little girl that poked so much fun at me this morning. Bouncing up and down, acting as if she had never humiliated me. My spirits were broken this morning but I intend to make up for my lack of self-esteem before. They plow off the bus, one by one. Trailing the two over blissful children is Grace Anne. The bus pulls away ear splitting as always. I can barely hear my own thoughts. I strain over the noise. "Hey Grace Anne!" as the noise level comes back to normal I shout again, just in case she didn't hear me. "Grace!" She turns around and screams.

"Anchor! Arrrrr Matey!" finding joy in herself. She smiles and I blush. Damn it. The redness, warm burning. What is this?

"How's the ship deck? Scrubbed clean is it? Don't wanna walk the plank do yah?" she says in a fit of laughter.

Chance is cracking up and Aria has a look on her face, like she told me so. I gather my thoughts and try to come up with a witty comeback but all I could force out. "Funny. No really You're funny. What was school like?" Instantly regretting my question.

She replies "Haven't you experienced school before?

"Well yes but.. Never mind. What year are you? What do you do after?" Shut up Anchor too many questions. I scold myself. She counters. "I work, do homework and then I sleep. You?"

"Is that where you were yesterday? Or were you just avoiding your future husband?"

At this point I just want to bite through my tongue, to cut off the chance of ever saying anything to this girl again. What the hell is my

Refuse to Sink

problem? She looks at me puzzled and explains. "Um no... I was at the Parks and Recreations of Maine. Trying to locate my mother. But she is at the Riviere De Loup in Quebec. That's about one hundred and twenty miles from here. So I probably wont see her for a few days. She rides the trains, so I don't know." she looks concerned.

"So after that I went to the grocery store to pick up food, to make for the remaining Keats." she snaps.

"Wow, you are how old?" I say slyly. My conscience patting me on the back, for sneaking the question in. "I am eighteen in four days." she says lightly.

I can feel my inner most Anchor jumping up and down at this news! My cheeks burn and I feel sweat drip down my neck, onward to my back and catch on my briefs. It is great news, possibly the best outcome. I follow her like a lost dog, hanging on her every word. Like it's the last thing I will ever hear her say. We reach her porch and I hear snoring from the inside. "Is that your dad?" I ask.

"Either that or one of the three bears has come home and realized that 'Goldie Locks' aka Aria, has eaten all the porridge"

She says with a laugh, as the door slams behind her. "I'll see you around Anchor." she yells from behind the screen door as she tosses her bag to the counter. I hear her father stirring and then fall back into a blissful drunken rest. I don't understand her calm, almost subdued attitude towards me. Usually, the females fall at my feet. Never this un appreciation. Maybe she's a master of deflection? And she wants me just as bad, just very good at hiding it? I shutter at the thought that she may just think I'm not very interesting. Then I decide to give being suave a another chance. "I guess I'll be seeing you soon my dear." I respond quickly and without thought obviously.

Really? My dear, what am I eighty or someone out of a horribly scripted movie? I really need to rethink my approach here. I need to go home and regroup. That's it, that's all. I'm a little off my game, which I agree is no excuse for acting like Charlie Chaplin on crack. But hey, there will always be tomorrow and tomorrow I will be Brad Pitt. I just know it.

I turn back just to complete this poor excuse for a meet- cute. I see her glancing out the compact kitchen window, watching me walk away. We lock eyes, she doesn't look away. I feel like this is my chance to prove I am not loco. That I am indeed smooth. Before I can stop myself. I shoot her two finger guns and wink. In a moment of shear disgrace. I turn around, trying to forget that I just damaged the chance of ever looking cool in front of this girl, again. In a haze of disappointment and confusion I turn around and BLAM! I run right into a light post that came out of nowhere, just to ruin my day. I stumble and fall to the ground in hopes that I would die from a head injury. Seems fitting. Since I will never again have to show my face around here. Before I know it. My mother has crouched by my side with a wet rag that reeks of cold chicken and bad lettuce. I shoo her away with her damp rag of infection. And try to sit up. All the while bating away the blue birds crowding my vision. Laughter fills the air ,once occupied by my cocky karma. Its Grace Anne. She is laughing at me, again. At least I accomplished that. My mother asked what happened. I hear Grace Anne say with pleasure. "I think he was imitating The Fonz. And it backfired."

I am drowning in a pool of my own embarrassment. After the dizziness wore, off I set up. Shook off the remaining dignity I had left then proceeded to walk solemnly back into the house. Grace laughed on her way back to her house. I didn't look back. I dare not repeat my ignorance. I pondered moving away, going to college in another town or state. I don't know how to talk to her. Let alone be around her again, after my utter shame and misfortune. But I have a job to do. I have to make her love me. And if that meant looking like a fool everyday for the rest of my life, than that's what I was prepared to do.

For the next few days, I met her every morning at the bus. We talked about what we did and occasionally about school or work, exchanged numbers and spoke over the phone. She always has nice stories. Stories of books that she loves and fantasies of becoming the worlds finest gardener. Having books written about her life and one day retiring to Maui. Not because she loves Hawaii, but just because she likes to say "Maui." She dreams of castles in the sky. I think that's how the saying goes? Which means she dreams much bigger than life. Which is never a bad thing. Most people walk this earth with one thought. Make it through. I have been one of those people and she refreshes me. Its easy to put limits on yourself. Get a job. A house. A family. Not her she is set to do great things and isn't afraid to let you know about it. Daily.

Refuse to Sink

D. C. Garriott

Chapter Seven

Grace Anne's favorite thing to do is to text funny faced, picture messages. The first time, she sent me a photo of her thumb up her nose from her Spanish class. Then a picture of her picking Ryan Goslings nose on a life size poster of him, at the theater were she worked. I think she has a thing for picking noses. I remember a quote my dad used to say. "Its okay to pick your nose, Its okay to pick your friends. But its not okay to pick your friends nose!" I always laughed, even though I thought is was possibly the stupidest thing I had ever heard. But none the less, it is relevant here.

Eventually, I could carry on a conversation with Grace Anne without bumbling and bringing up weird facts, statistics or old cartoons she knew nothing about. I would spout off random information about our state, that you wouldn't even have to go to school to know. Just pick up a brochure. But I for some reason, thought it would impress her like. "Did you know Portland was considered the Foodiest small town in America by Bon Appétit magazine? Why would I be reading Bon Appetite magazine? Well if you have to ask, you haven't been paying attention to my mothers personality. It was often located directly in front of the toilet.

"Or that internationally known classical artists visit Blue Hill to train every summer at Kneisel Hall? Also the state has the largest bear population in the lower 48?" Jesus Christ, it flows out of my mouth like hot lava. She always laughs with me. I don't know if she is laughing at me,or with me. But I am sure of one thing, she is laughing. A lot. And smiling. I love this. I crave it and try not to see it, when I close my eyes. She lives beneath my eye lids. When I close them, she appears replacing the nightmares of my fathers death.

I lay in a delicate garden of daisy's with her re-enacting movie parts

Refuse to Sink

and reciting EE Cummings. I believe he is one of the most influential poets ever. Keep in mind that these are dreams, not real life. I can't seem to get close enough to her to do these things in real life through her busy schedule of being an adult. Grace Anne is responsible for the care of her sister and her alcoholic father. Cooking and cleaning in her mothers constant absence. I am pretty sure she didn't sign up for this willingly. But she takes on the task like a true pro. I bet she will make a great mother one day.

I have a hard enough time stopping my constant know it all opposite personality, that I have developed since I met her to explain to her anything but useless information.

I see her everyday at the bus stop. I could have stopped walking my brother there days ago, since he now felt comfortable with the route. But I continue to join him in hopes of building a strong friendship with this girl. Everyday I grow more confident in my pursuit. I ask her about her family her home country. Even though she was born here, she has a lot of information about the country her mother hails from. I try to act interested and avoid staring at her with lustful eyes. "Colombia is beautiful, the plants are way prettier there I think. Have you ever been to another country?"

She is self contained and powerful when she speaks. Her obsession with nature is significant, she speaks with such intelligence and knows just about every kind of flower or weed. I begin to realize, that she is way smarter than me. "Um. No I have been to Alabama once and trust me it's like another country. They sometimes don't even speak good English! Right doesn't have a Y in it. Just saying." She giggles and begins to sound out the Y in right. Everyday I ask her to hang out with me, some days she obliges and some days I watch her work her fingers to the bone, to make due of what her mother left undone.

We relax on a blanket in my backyard after school, watching our young siblings play catch. The shade drips off the overly large Cat Spruce Tree, creating a river of dim light around us. We indulge in the protection from the sun. I laugh at her when she trips on a tree stump, she makes fun of my "Pirate" name.She sings. "Yo -ho-ho"and "Shiver me timber!" Making ridiculous references to HOOK.

It is a natural thing now to flirt. She touches my face and I grab her waist and tickle her soft, almost perfect stomach. We are comfortable with each other, without becoming too forward. I enjoy her. She

D. C. Garriott

obviously notices me as a boy. Finally. But I was beginning to feel a little friend zoned. That is a devastating feeling, when you are in woe of a woman. The "Friend Zone" is a dangerous ledge to walk on. It is the thin line between a hug, and sex. A hi five and a kiss. And once established, is hard to erase. I will not be friend zoned. I have to get her in my direct path, without risking the "too forward" Anchor reemerging. This is a task for me since I just want to grab her face and soak her lips against mine. What if she were to pull away? What if its to soon? *Patience Anchor.*

Grace Anne spends a lot of time keeping up her appearance as head of the household, on account of her mother being distant and her father being a complete waste of space. I wondered how she had such a great perspective on life. When most other children would fall right in line with the cycle. And by the cycle I mean. Your mother or father acts like an ass. Then in turn, you act like an ass. Point blank this "Cycle" happens everyday in America and beyond. Children mimic what they see, there's no gray area. Its black and white, ether you change yourself or you turn into your parents. Then your children turn into you.

Before we know it, we've got a whole population of short fused, assholes. Not Grace though, she is very centered on not letting herself nor her sister, get swept away in the negative air she breathes everyday. I believe she thinks her smile is a force field against it. Maybe it is. I begin to loathe Grace Anne's father immediately.

I wondered how he got this way and made a million excuses in my head about how he came to be this disgusting excuse for a human being. Let alone a father. Buck was a fisherman, he worked at the sea ports for ten years. One day the manager stumbled upon him asleep on the ship deck, with a broken string net and no catches for the day. He wasn't fired on the spot. He was fired the third time they caught him. The man that fired him was his own father. He was written off as a disgrace. It was his last chance to prove himself due to the Army discharge. Which upset his father, beyond all reconciliation.

Also marrying a "Cuban" as they called Flora, Grace Anne's mother. Colombian. That's her race. But that didn't matter to them. She was indeed foreign and that's all she would ever be. It's amazing by the looks of him now that he could ever even find a woman like that to be his wife. He is not near tall enough, or attractive enough. He has long stringy brown hair that hits his shoulders and scuffled beard, that doesn't look like he has shaved in years. His eyes black and scary, like a troll of

Refuse to Sink

some sort. Grace Anne's mother Flora is just as pretty as her daughters. I got a glimpse of her, on one of her short trips home. She was standing on the porch smoking a cigarette and talking on the phone. Her hair flowed just like Grace Anne's. Flora had specks of gray in hers and it seemed to shimmer like silver when the sun hit it. She had the prettiest smile and an accent that I'm sure drove every man that graced her presence, half crazy. She winked at me, when she noticed me watching innocently and instantly I was embarrassed. I am sure the girls received no features from their repelling father.

He doesn't blink often when I'm around. I don't know if he doesn't trust me, or people in general. Grace Anne was vague when answering my "Why did Buck get kicked out of the military?" questions. "Something about anger issues and a fight?" she replied briskly and changed the subject immediately. It always seemed kind of weird to me that she didn't know very much about the man that has been basically raising her, through the drunken spells and the switching of jobs every other month due to the latter.

Grace Anne had developed a close bond with her younger sibling Aria. With the lack of parental guidance, this is to be expected. She was the mother and father. She went to her school plays and was very involved with her academics. Resulting in Aria being at the top of her class. I was intimidated by the fact that she cared so much. Even though it was a similar story to mine, except much worse.

I taught my brother how to ride a bike and put a worm on a hook. But his homework was his. I had other things to do. Then again I did have a mother. And I feel sad that I wasn't there enough, like Grace Anne. She is an angel. Does she have *any* bad behaviors? Quirks? I want to know. I doubt it. But all people do. I have this thing, where I repeat what I've said in my head to check and see if its witty or smart enough. Like an inner spell check of sorts. Which been strangely absent recently. Or the thing I do with my tongue. I click it excessively, if I'm nervous. I say "Sorry" even when its not necessary to say.

Here I stand yet again, kicking dust and rocks around when bus 532 pulls up at 3:05 exactly. Thank god. I couldn't last another minute. The little ones crash off the bus with stories that fall on deaf ears, because all I hear is Grace saying.

"Hey aren't you supposed to be at work?" her smiles sets my face on fire. "Huh? Oh no, not today. I have something to show you." she looks at my

D. C. Garriott

hands. "Oh its not something it's somewhere." She looks interested. "I don't have to work, but do have homework times two, will it take long?" "No No not long. We will be back before dinner!"

She is sold, she guides her sister in to get a snack. She returns to the porch, wearing the shortest shorts I have ever seen. I have seen pretty girls in short shorts, but none that drove me into a frenzy like this. It takes all I have to stop myself from staring and pick up my jaw. I follow her around the side of my "new" truck that is circa 1987. Can you use "Circa" when referring to the 80's. I don't know, but it might as well have been from the 1800's. It is elderly, but tough looking and I think it makes my image a little more rustic or dangerous maybe? No, probably not. I open the door to the passenger side, she hops in and we are off.

I have previously put a picnic basket in the back, full of stuff for our little trip. I hope she doesn't think its lame, which is a constant thought of mine these days. We ride for fifteen minutes. She is talking about her day and her Spanish teacher riding her about volunteering this summer at camp. I ask her a few questions about this summer what she plans on doing and her college plans, she responds excitedly.

"I am moving..." This crushes me instantly. She continues "New York City, I have an apartment and everything, just waiting for me to graduate." I fight the thousand of questions to the back of my mind. Like "What is her problem?" "What is wrong with Caribou?" "Does she know how dangerous it is for a young girl there?" After the manic questions in my head cease. I carry on with the conversation. "Really? What will you do there?"

" I will be working with the State Parks and Recs, just like my mom. Grounds keeper mostly. Then work my way up the ladder." she says with pride. "I don't know if I could work around pollen like that. I sneeze at a daisy!" I laugh at myself. Thinking back to the dandelion in my dream of my father.

We arrive at our destination. She looks surprised and amused. The winds wisp the sandy beach. The sun shines down and produces a shimmer across the rocks. "Anchor what are we doing?"

"We are having a picnic." I respond. Her eyes light up and then squint at me. "You trying to woe me?" I smile. "Yes ma'am" I tip an imaginary hat, that seems to amuse her fully. As I grab the basket and blanket out of the truck bed, she grabs my arm and pulls it tight to her side. Other than my brain feeling like its going to explode, its the best feeling I have ever felt.

Refuse to Sink

I silently prayed we would never reach the sand. But we do, to my dismay. The sand releases below my sandals and embraces the soles of my feet. She releases. I feel remorse, but try not to let her know how displeased I am. "You know Central Park is the best piece of landscaping work I have ever seen. And I don't see anything but grass, flowers and falling in love in my head." she calmly says.

"Butterflies and Rainbows you mean?" I say with a sarcastic laugh. "Ha! You mock me." her laughter intoxicating.

"No, not at all. I mean falling in Love is dangerous." Grace looks at me with a look of disappointment and anger and exclaims. "I have a feeling you are full of shit." I start to laugh. "Wow you got some language!" she smiles shyly. "I'm not as innocent as I look, boy."

I wonder what she means by this? I mean no virginal girl could ever pull off jean shorts like that. *She must be hitting on me?* My fragile little mind can't handle this pressure. I reach over her to grab the butter knife for the cheese and with dramatic effect; I linger. If she wants to kiss me this is the moment for it. Instead, she gets as close to my lips as humanly possible. I feel her warm breath that smells like a mixture of plums and butterscotch. And she whispers. "Your being very dangerous.."

Indeed I was. And I liked it. It's like playing with fire, its all fun and entertaining until you get burned. And that shit hurts for days.

♫

D. C. Garriott

Chapter Eight

It is restful there on the beach. Our conversation carries on without any awkward moments. Its so easy to talk to her, to touch her. I feel good around her and she feels at ease. I watch her as she walks to the edge of the water. She bends down to pick up a rock and sends it skipping across the surface. She turns back and catches my stare. The setting sun shines around her hair and produces a halo. *Has my father sent her to me?* I ponder and quickly dismiss. I have a hard time with divine intervention.

"Hey do you think we could do this again, tomorrow?" I ask as we are packing up the remnants of our little playful picnic. "I don't know as of now if I have to work, but maybe we can catch a movie or just hang for a bit tomorrow at your house?" Absolutely. I nod. Then regretfully show her the way back to my truck.

As we are walking up the hill back to my truck. I begin to feel this feeling that I cant control. I drop the basket,grab her under her arms and toss her up in the air and she lands in my arms. She faces me and shouts. "What was that for?" I look at her longing for our lips to touch, she leans in and lays the sweetest most genital kiss on the tip of my nose. I am sure from the previous meeting on the shore that it will lead to more. But it doesn't. She smiles and says. "Are you gonna carry me the whole way? Because I will let you." I did.

We spent the whole drive home,talking about our past,the town I came from and past loves. What they did wrong and what we didn't. She glances at me. I glance at her. I turn up the radio, she sings under the volume her voice is so precious. Listening to her causes my heart to move up in my throat. I have never been so intoxicated by someone. I think back to Shakespeare, and wonder if this is the feeling that lead those two young children to literally, bury themselves in love. It was young puppy love at its best. You know, the kind of love that makes everything make sense and no sense all, at the same time. The feeling in

Refuse to Sink

your stomach when you touch. The way the world stood still the minute you saw them. Very poetic right?She is my world, my capture, my heart. My infatuation was more than sexual. But it was about sex. I wanted to know her that way, but I would be willing to wait forever. Because the sex we have with our eyes, was well enough for now.

As we arrive at her driveway. I see Chance and Aria playing in a make-shift sand box. Jumping around. I guess playing cops and robbers but who knows. Before I could get around to the passenger side door, Grace had already exited the cab. "I am still carrying you right? Angel's feet never touch the ground."

Normally I would feel like an ass hole for the lamest comment ever made towards a female. Again reconnecting with Romeo. With one quick swoop, she is again off the ground. She is lighter than a feather. I love lifting her up. It feels good in my bones. It makes me feel strong and proud. Its really overwhelming the amount of heat I feel for this girl! But this time she looks embarrassed, even scared. I set her down promptly. The spirit of the beach has faded. She is serious Grace Anne again. Yelling for her sister, telling her its time to eat and to get cleaned up. She turns to me, laying her hand on my face so softly. "I just don't want my father to get angry, you understand right?" I did understand. I nod. Her eyes melt my disappointment away. I am lost in a daze for a moment. Mind control is real folks. I may have a vampire on my hands here. I laugh to myself I as shake the thought from my feeble mind. I close her door and head for my driveway. My brother in toe, asking a bunch of kissing questions and sneering at my lack of answers.

When I lay my head down that night. I am filled with anxiety. I am going to have to tell her about my father. I have chosen to omit this information, when I heard her love for New York. If she doesn't already know. Which I doubt. The only information she might get would be from my brother and I bet that's not the sort of thing ten year old children talk about during patty cake. "Oh and FYI my father was brutally murdered." Oh no, not something to be spoke of at recess. That's the making of nightmares, most kids try to avoid those..

I drift off to sleep, which seems to take hours. I think about how I will approach this, the answer is clear. Hold my head up high and just tell her. The heat of the morning is unusual, its normally very brisk. My brother and I opt for no jackets. Its Friday. Chance is excited for the weekend and I am as well. Grace Anne comes strolling out, as she does

D. C. Garriott

every morning and greets me with a wink and a smile she says. "I do not have to work, but I will be going to the theater tonight anyways."
Why is she going there and not with me. I don't understand my heart strings begin to pull and I struggle to keep my cool. "You did ask me to go correct?" my pulse returns to a normal pace. "Why yes, I did do that. So what do you say 8 o'clock?"

"Meet me here after school and I will take you around town first and show you around okay?" She says with the prettiest smile I have ever seen, and my knees buckle. "I'll be right here waiting" I stop talking at this point and just enjoy the fact that she still wants to hang around me after so many infractions in our brief, for lack of a better word. Relationship. I might be getting better at this whole wooing thing. I will woe her. I will woe the shit out of her! Until there is no chance, she would or could choose another over me. No lop sided banter for me this morning. I am not gonna mess this up.

The children and my Grace Anne load onto the bus. I glance towards where she is sitting, my eyes lock with hers. I feel the connection so strong. She gets me. Respects me. Needs me. I'll ask her to marry me one day. And if there's a God in heaven, she will agree.

I set off to the Shorelines. I have landed an interview at the shrimp docks. I pass by a harbor and smile at the sight of Puffins hanging about and donning their black and white tuxedos. Bouncing up and down imitating their nickname. "Clowns of the Sea" When I reach the docks. I am confronted by a stronger than hulk man, who introduces himself as Mary Adams. I chuckle immediately. He makes a face and says. "Yes it's Mary. As in laugh at my name again and I'll kick your ass." I digress. He continues.

"You will be down there Anchor." he says with a hint of sarcasm. "Yes Sir… I mean Ma'am.. I'm mean Sir.." I laugh just to assure him that I am indeed, not afraid of his fist.

"Just get down there before you are late and just a word of advice, wear something a little less gay tomorrow." Smiling at his own boastful attitude. I shake my head in confusion. Realizing I am still wearing Chances colorful macaroni necklace, he made me from school. Shit.

The job isn't hard but definitely boring. You put the line in the bay, you bring the line out of the bay. You pick the little bitty shrimp out and anything else that gets caught. I have seen diapers (used) tons of beer

49

Refuse to Sink

cans also a small coyote that seemed to wonder one step to close to the wrong side of the dock. Stupid animal. You gather at lunch time and realize that men may gossip more than women. But without all the pearls and sugar cubes of course. Then you go back to the line, pull in, then back out again. Before I know it three o'clock strikes. I rush off the docks and pass "Mother Mary". That one earned me a punch so hard to the shoulder today. I am pretty sure my humerus bone is bruised. Ironic? Yes.

Jumping in my truck, my foot hits the peddle. I spin out of the gravel and down the road. Letting the wind hit me in the face appreciating that it wasn't Mary. Catching my idle hands waving at the puffins as if we are old friends.

I find myself lingering by the road, waiting. My mother had given me the go ahead to romp and play with my new "friend". She doesn't get off work until five. So the movie I plan on taking her too, has to wait until then. The bus doors open and with it, a familiar sight, the two children heave off the bus with all their energy. And behind them, comes Grace Anne. Smiling as usual and glimmering with the amazing superpower to disable all thoughts, that don't involve the smell of her hair or the tightness of that shirt she's wearing.

"Ready?" she says as excited as me I presume.

Her hair wishing in the breeze, eyes sparkling with the light of the sun. "Mom doesn't get off till five. But we can chill at my house till then?" I respond.

"Chill… Anchor? Really you need to step out of the 90's and back to our world!" She laughs always at my expense it seems. I return a chuckle and grab her around the waist. Its small, yet full. And feels amazing in my palms. "Yes Chill…. Or make out? Or watch TV?" I say with a hint of ego.

"Let me check on my house first and then I'll be over" she replies with a smile.

I rush back to the house to clean up the awfulness I call my room. Before I can finish, she is knocking on my door. Of course, she has changed into a pair of tight jeans that leave less to the imagination than the shorts from yesterday. I don't complain, because the neon green shirt fits the whole outfit like a glove. Her belly button is now playing peek a boo with my libido. We set down on my bed. Its all I can do not to push her back and rip the clothes off as quickly as she put them on.

D. C. Garriott

Hormones are the devil. We sit and talk about the same things school, the weather. My mind races. I keep drawing my eyes away from her mid section, so she doesn't think I'm some kind of pervert. Which I am. But I don't want her to know this. At least not yet. I smile at my devious thoughts when I catch her picking up a picture of my father and I at the beach. Sitting atop of my dresser.

She asked what happened to him. "Divorce?" she asks with no smile. I wanted to say divorce. But then I'd be lying and I never want to lie to her. "No, death." I say sadly.

"Really? How did he die?" I sigh. "He was murdered." "Holy crap Anch! Why didn't you tell me?" she cries out. "This is a ridicules thing. Not to mention, don't you think?"

"Um not a huge conversation starter. Hey my names Anchor. My father was killed via gun shot to the heart on the streets of New York City!"I blurt out.

When the words New York City hit the air, it turns cold and her face turns a shade of red. I wanted to suck the words back in. Make up a new destination, to where he was shot. But for the life of me I couldn't recall any other city at that moment. I sit stunned for a minute, mulling it over in my head. How in the hell did I ruin the mood so fast. But that's what death does, it ruins things.

"New York, Anchor? That's where it happened?" she bellows.

I feel the anxiety building and I try to change the tone. But the torment pushes through. My face feels like its swelling. It is anger? Anxiety? Or sadness? Whatever ever it was. It was causing me to raise the tone of my voice. "Yes, the one with all the pretty parks and attractions. My father worked there. He was mugged and killed for twenty bucks." I continue. "You know its dangerous there Grace, and you plan on going alone and that scares me half to death!" I am pretty sure I am yelling at this point my ears have the familiar feel of water filling up in them, I can no longer hear correctly.

She straightens her back and raises up off the bed with a mix of remorse and optimism. She stands next to me shoulder to shoulder, we both look at the photo.

Grace Anne reaches around my waist and gives a slight tug to my shirt. It feels like comfort. "I never really saw myself strolling through Central Park, eating a bagel and deciding which Broadway Show I would attend"

Refuse to Sink

I say sarcastically. Grace Anne releases my lower back and pushes me away playfully.

"Really? that's what you see when you think of the City? A sarcastic version maybe, and I feel like I'm being mocked." She says with a frown. "Its highly Sarcastic. And what's so good about it? Its dangerous and dirty and they think that big green park and the bright lights apparently impress most people. I am not impressed"

"Are you not impressed Anchor? Or are you scared of the"Bright lights?" I can see why they would blind you. But you don't have to be afraid of it because of your father."

I cant help but look at her with aggravation. Even though, I could never stay mad at her. "You speak so much about things you know nothing about Grace. And its a little disturbing" She looks at me with disbelief. As if no one has ever stood up to her in this way. She politely smiles.

"I'm so sorry Anch. But not everybody dies in the city. What happened to your dad, was a terrible fluke and there's no doubt it was ugly and messy but that should in no way stop you from discovering the rest of your life."

"Nobody ever dies in the City? That's what your saying to me? Well, I already know one person who did and that's not the best odds my dear friend." I counter. She plops back down on the bed in disgust. Her brows are now cocked downward, her sweet glossy lips puckered.

"No they Don't!(her sympathy fading) NO! It's where people go to be alive, to feel something, a dream, a hope and a future. And that's where I am going to find mine!" I join her on the bed. Sitting down close to her. I reach out and embrace her frame.

"You're so cute, with all your talks of dreams and a better life. I think you've read one to many Young Adult Novels." I say with a crooked grin. "Let me guess, you will be saved by Spider Man. Or fall madly in love with a street painter and you can write about all your adventures and make millions!"

"Your an ass hole. And yes I like that scenario." She pulls away. We both have a laugh.

Grace Anne leans over, getting incredibly close to my face as she has done before. I feel her lips move against mine. "Seriously Anch. You talk about life like you know what your saying is the truth. But your eyes have this constant expression of confusion. Its like your brain is telling your face, that you have no clue"

I slowly reach my hand around her waist, which is a natural habit when a woman is this close to my face. I can feel the passion, my hand slides around and up the back of her shirt. Softly. I caress the lower part of her naked back. And just as the air between us begins to warm back up. The front door slams, with a bit of unnecessary force. I realize my mother is announcing herself, as to not interrupt anything. We jump back stunned and raise up off the bed in a hurry, to greet my tired mother. She is standing in the kitchen with her hands on her hips, like she is trying to remember something. "Hello Mrs. Aldwin" Grace Anne says politely and my mother smiles. "Please call me Wynna. What times the movie? You two crazy kids" I shake my head at her, begging her not to say anything so lame, that I may have to go blow my head off.

"Less than an hour we better get going!" I answer.
The ride to the movie theater is filled with music and laughter. I explain to her that I haven't "seen" a movie in years. Yes. I used finger quotes. She proposes to me, we will be "watching" this one. She mocks me with her own finger quotations. Grace Anne goes on to give me a synopsis of the "Chick flick" she is Not dragging me to see. Even though I would have rather watched something more action packed. Or at the least deeper than a fabricated love story that will most likely, make me look like an asshole in the end.

You know those movies that are just plan unattainable. Yet, these woman will base their entire lives on the fictional bullshit, that lonely authors write to make us all look stupid and UN-knightly. Whatever. I just think that when you are writing a love story, lets try and make it somewhat believable. Then men everywhere, might have a chance against these odds and so many marriages wont fail, so fast. You got to love that none of these woman put down in the divorce papers: Not Noah Calhoun, or Edward Cullen.

"Irreconcilable differences." That is horseshit, and they know it. I undeniably, hate Channing Tatum. First of all, what is with that name? Makes my mind wonder, thinking that there is a laboratory somewhere in Russia, that is creating these robot like male romance stars. I have to say, my inner Anchor believes, if someone were to rip their faces off we would undoubtedly have ourselves a Terminator moment.

Refuse to Sink

D. C. Garriott

<u>*Chapter Nine*</u>

She smells of crisp melon. The wind hits her and the scent flows onto my face. I can only imagine what she must taste like. I get a streak of cold chills just thinking about it. Probably watermelon or sweet grapes. I want to find out. She catches me looking at her and not the road, she smacks me on the arm, drawing my eyes back to the road and my thoughts back to middle school. She smacked me…. Awesome. When we arrive at the theater. I make sure that I show her my chivalry. By opening her door. And hope that this will not have to live up to the "Prince" in the movie, we are about to see.

The anticipation of the lights falling over the theater, and getting the all too famous first kiss from my leading lady is making my heart beat fast and my breath shorten. We reach the theater galley. Grace Anne exchanges "Hello's" and "How have you been's" To the people she sees waiting in line. Then to her friends, that work in the theater. She is obviously very popular and admired. A couple of the males almost look disappointed at the sight of us. Of course, they are trying hard to look unaffected by the whole thing. But clearly man to man, they were pissed. As they should be. Because I am with the girl, everyone seems to want to be with.

I stand proudly next to her my eyes warning the gentlemen. I throw my arm around her shoulders, for good measure. She accepts my gesture and places her arm around my side, grabbing my belt loop. This sends shivers up my spine yet again. I let go of her,in fear that my excitement may show. *There*. A look of confusion crosses her face then is dismissed when she turns to the clerk. "What cha up to sis?" A young woman says behind the counter. "We want to see **Come Away With Me** the 8:30 showing please, doll. " Grace Anne institutes. My eyes roll with out warning. She glares at my exposed disposition, her eye brows low, then turns back to the young lady.

55

Refuse to Sink

"Well you just made it. And who is the lovely fella, you have with you?" she says in a flirty fashion.

Grace Anne throws her head back and laughs "Mandie! This is my future husband... didn't you know?" The girl looks puzzled and replies. "Okay then. I believe you have lost your mind and here are your tickets to "Bat Shit Crazy" she laughs. We all laugh. But only I know. Grace Anne is pointing fun at the first comments I made to her.

We retrieve the necessities for a good movie, popcorn, drink, and candy. Sour Patch Kids. If you don't get them, you are a fool. They are splendid. We make our way to the dark room with the big screen, and find a seat in the back where most "lovers" do. As we sit and wait for the movie to begin, we talk nervously about the up coming flicks and what tomorrow will bring. When the lights fall dark my mind goes wild, because its technically the first time I've ever been in the dark with Grace Anne.

My body has reacted to the pleasure of the unknown. I try hard to hide my excitement placing the popcorn in my lap. I drift the box of candy on to her lap. Gracefully floating my hand across her belly. I feel her jerk suddenly, but give no sign of wanting the advance to stop. Her breath quickens she takes a sip of the soda. Then places it on the other side of her as to make room for further advances. I linger on her stomach. When I feel the sensation of her heart beating fast. I follow the thumps up to her breast and lightly mold them with steady hands. If I know anything and have full confidence in, it is this. She begins to move her body into my hands. I follow the short breaths up to her lips. Beginning to caress them with the tips my fingers and before she can catch the next breath of excitement. I press my lips to hers. My lips are hot and desperate. Hers warm with intensity, pressed together then cascading to each others necks then back up to her mouth. The smell of her neck is intoxicating, sweet sugar coated nectar. Her lips plump, her lip gloss wet with confection. I grab her inner thigh and pull her legs apart, sliding my palm up and down her bare leg. I have to keep my body half way in my seat. This is a struggle of epic proportions. I want to lunge on her and feel what she feels like underneath me.

The coddling and massaging goes on for what seems like the length of the movie. It includes a lot of exploration of other parts of each our bodies, we would not dare touch in the daylight. But in the darkness of the movie theater, we discover each other in the innocent glow of this first experience. Her kiss is magical. It sends my thoughts into a frenzy. I cant focus on anything, but the way she smells and the way she taste How she thrust like she has done this before. Her innocence, is now in question. She has mastered the art of the first kiss. She does it better than I. Knowing I have had many more than her. I thought at one point, she was going to grab *it*. But she veered back to my chest to my disappointment.

After the movie was finished we try and recollect what small pieces of the film we actually watched in between bathing in each others sexuality. It seemed a bit awkward outside of the movie. Even though it is still dark out it seems the fear reemerged without the comfort of the that *kind* of darkness. On the ride home. I feel larger than life. I had gotten the kiss and much more. She's a pepper that girl. All the flirting and teasing has paid off big time. But now I want more a lot more. I am closer now, than I have ever been. I decide to speak, to end the awkward silence. "So when's the next time we can see a chick flick? That was amaze-balls." I question with a look of innocence. I rarely exude.

"I've seen better." She winks as she fixes her kiss soaked mouth in the mirror.

"Really? That is hard to believe I have been told that particular flick was the best many times." I reply with a hint of ego.
"Oh so you have seen that one before? So I'm not the first to take you to see it?" Grace Anne snaps back.

"Ha! Oh Gracie Poo you are the first to make a movie that interesting. Before I just watched and waited for it to be over. Never have I felt so.... you know.. Excited about it" I reply obvious like. She chuckles shyly. "Oh I know you were excited about that movie. There was no eye rolling during it." she snickers.
"None. More tongue rolling though. I think you are a beautiful kisser. I wouldn't mind that all the time." I explain with a lump forming in my throat. Crap. My nervousness has reared.

"Well that's good to know, so kiss me again and tell me goodnight because I am going to need that kiss to survive the up coming twilight." she says desperately.

"Absolutely my dear.... " I say warmly. I stop shortly in her drive way. I turn to her. She smiles, we lean in to make the sweet kiss last. It's as timeless as ever. Our bodies are burning hot with passion. This is new its romantic, not egotistical or vain. Nether is trying to show the other

Refuse to Sink

something new. Just pure sensuality. No need to impress or be impressed. She kisses my nose. I rub my hands through her hair and drift down to her back above her belt loop. Cascading my fingers down, gasping her bottom. She flinches then eases closer. Oh my, this girl is so awesome. My heart thumps so loudly in my head, pounding against two parts of my body. Just as I am reaching around to her "maternal connection". Through the bounty of love noises we are enjoying. We hear a gun shot.

D. C. Garriott

Chapter Ten

This ends the kiss and my excitement. We both jerk our necks around, to locate the direction in which the noise echoed. It is coming from Grace's house. What could be happening? Grace throws her hair up in a pony tail, we bound out of the truck. Grace wiping the moisture from her face. I tuck my hair under my hat. We enter the house to find a gaping hole in the wall of the Keatz family room. Aria has taken cover under the kitchen table in the distance, holding her blanket across her face only exposing her eyes. She looks terrified. Understandable, when your father is wielding a loaded gun. Mr. Keats stands, well stammers in one place pointing the gun at the family photo, that hangs above the black wood burning stove.

"That Cheating Whore!!!!!!!!!" he yells. "She's a real pa- pa- piece of work she is!" His voice so loud, it burns my ears. Buck stumbles backwards and falls to the chair. Another shot fires. He shoots a second hole in the wall. The walls are so thin, he could have very well punched the wall in with his fist. This gun is unneeded. I begin to think of ways to take him down. Going over the wrestling tricks, my father had taught me. He never told me how to take down a mad man though, with a gun and a drunken sense of super strength. He looks back at me, the look is cold and feels dead. Am I dreaming this too? If I am please, Anchor wake up! I will trade the good part of the dream, for Grace Anne's nightmare to end! WAKE UP! I come to grips with this being the reality, not a dream this time. I have to do something! I jump in front of Grace. I will defend her. I will defend this first kiss. I stare him down with desperate authority.

My legs shake beneath me. I can clearly see, this is angering him more. I wipe the sweat beads from my face, staring through his angered eyes. With such force I could feel my feet gripping the floor. Through my work boots."Who the Hell are you boy? That- that's that little punk Gracie? God you could do better stupid girl!" He shouts to Grace Anne.

59

Refuse to Sink

Cop sirens can be heard down the road. Grace Anne moves from behind me, she passes the drunken lunatic without fear. She grabs her sister from beneath the table and carries her rapidly out the back door, towards my mother. And the stand off is over, as the police burst into the living room, throwing Buck to the floor. This will not end well. Really makes you think how angry would you have to be to disregard your children health or quality of life? I couldn't ever imagine hurting or scaring my little brother or mother in this way? I could never think of it, for my own child.

My mother had already began making her way across the yard between our two houses. I dash behind Grace Anne, never losing the painful eye contact with the man wielding a deadly weapon behind us. My mother is in so much fright. She examines my torso and head, to see if I had been shot. Her eyes bursting with tears.

"I only witnessed the second shot in person. I am fine." I assured her. She backed off, cleared her face. Then turns to Aria. She is unharmed other than a slight bruise to her left eye, she said she got it when she was trying to keep her father from grabbing the gun out of the closet. My mother grabs a bag, throws ice in it; then places it on Aria's cheek. Just like a good mother would. I really think my mother would have done well as a mother to a daughter. I watch her with Aria. She has such a sweet nature to her. She would've understood all the ups and down of the "Womanly Hormone rages." I think she was hoping for a girl when Chance came along, but she would never say it. Just a bunch of " As long as its healthy." Ha. Right.

What an ordeal this night has turned out to be. I feel a little selfish of my glorious encounter earlier. My little brother awakes and is inquiring to what just happened, talking to Aria like they were old friends. Always solid, he tells her. "It will be alright Aria, don't worry." This is not true of course, because not twenty seconds later Mr. Keatz is hand cuffed and ushered out into a police car. He will probably not return to their home anytime soon. As for their mother. I am not sure where she went, but I am sure by her fathers exclamations. That she is also gone for good, with someone else.

My mother offers to let the two frightened girls stay at our house, they don't resist. My mother lays them out cot like beds on our living room floor. Aria is shaken although not harmed, she is still fragile. My mother speaks to the Emergency Response Team. "Its okay they can stay here tonight. They are shaken and could benefit from people they know. Tell the Child Services people, they can pick them up in the morning." Her voice still trembling with fright but very assertive. Very matter of fact. They took her seriously. They had to!

I follow Grace Anne to her house, to get their things for school the next day. She tries to piece together what probably happened tonight. She explained that her mother was a "free spirit" and is in and out so much, that she barely knows who she is. Also she has about ten steady boyfriends, who never seemed to mind that she was married, with two children. She doesn't speak very good English. So she used that as a way to not obey the sanity of marriage. Let alone honor her duties as a mother. She stares off in to the dim light of the holey living room. Looking at a picture of just her, Aria and her mother. The sand is wet beneath them and the sun sets across the water. She speaks in a whisper. "You see my father is not in this picture?"
"Yes I see." I reply, not knowing where this is going.
"My mother left him two years ago, she took us off to Florida. We stayed in a house meant for two, that sustained at least eight including us." She continued to clarify, that her mother had taken off with them to her mothers house in Miami, Florida.

Her grandmother housed other Colombian refugees. "It felt like we were on the outside looking in because we understood just about half of what the people were saying. It was not a good experience." she shakes her head. "I cant imagine." I say gently.
"NO… NO you couldn't, you don't know what that life is like. The broke life. The not eating, awful mother, asshole father life!"

Indeed. I did not know what having an awful mother was like. But I did know what it was like to have no father and a broken family. But at the least I had strudel to fill my aching belly. And a mother to defend me. To protect me. She is showing the heart on her sleeve, for the first time. I see her pain through those big hazel eyes. I begin to hurt for her. I love her. I truly and madly love this little star that fell down from the bright night sky for me. This is the first time I have ever heard her raise her voice. And it is towards me. What did I do? I walk towards her, she steps away. "Gracie," I say faintly, as I feel a rush of air leaving my body.
"I'm sorry, I yelled at you. I didn't mean that Anch. I just get so damn angry at them!" she places her hand to my cheek, its flushed with outrage yet still soft as ever.

Refuse to Sink

She looks down at the ground and says with a hint of sadness. "I think she only married that man, for a green card. Thus, glorifying the stereotype I live with everyday." I choose not to talk anymore. I grab her waist pulling her close to me. She wraps her arms around my chest and buries her face in to it, like a small child. We linger there for what seems like fifteen minutes, she finds the rhythm in my heart beat and begins to sway back and forth to it. I place my fingers under her chin and pull her face to mine. We share an innocent kiss. I grab her hand and lead her out the door, away from the scene that affects her heart so much.

Reaching my house I smell something familiar. It couldn't be? My mother yelps at my brother in a motherly tone to sit down and finish his plate,or no dessert. Dessert? Really? Grace Anne glances at my expression and realizes I am pleased.

"What are you so happy about?" questions as we enter the house. "Do you smell that? That is my mothers famous Strudel. You have to taste these decadent puffs of awesomeness!" I shout with child-like tone.

"Okay.. Okay Charlie! Calm down!" she laughs. "Charlie?"I question. Could she have called me by another mans name. Really? After what I've shown her today. I am sure she will never even recall another mans name.

"In the Chocolate Factory??" Grace Anne is now in full on laughter, my mother joins in with her by the time I can catch up the whole kitchen is busting with hilarity. "Well Golly Grace" bowing my head. "I guess you got me there."

As we enter the kitchen, my mother smiles, handing a dessert plate to Grace. Chance and Aria are already occupying the two chairs surrounding the small cafe table. They are laughing and talking. "What are you all talking about?" I ask. Chance responds. "You and Grace. And your little love roller coaster." Grace blushes and looks away towards her little sister who stares back at her with hopeful eyes. Already smiling again. It's amazing the power those strudels have.

"I hear Anchor is quite the musician? Singer are we?" Aria announces.

"Yes, he is Aria." My mother speaks for me.

"I am no musician. I can play piano, and only sing to myself. Why even talk about this… Its weird." I snap at them.

Grace glances at my reddened cheeks and professes. "Oh you can sing? Wow Anchor! I must here something. Like now. This is too good! Please!" Her eyes sparkle with anticipation.

62

D. C. Garriott

"I don't think so. Mom, why did you bring this up?" I say with an embarrassed smile. But she is nowhere to be found. I here her shuffling stuff around in the hallway closet. "Oh look what I salvaged from home…" she presents my old key board and stand and begins to set it up in front of me. CRAP.

"I haven't played in weeks!" I stammer out in fright. Looking around the room. They all stare at me. Aria nudges my arm. And I decide to set down and go for it. Because if I don't. I will let down this entire kitchen. Like I said. I can play. But stage fright gets the best of me sometimes. I freeze and panic. One of the reasons I didn't jump right into the music academy in New York. That and I hate new york. But that's neither here nor there.

"What are you gonna play, Son?" my mother questions. "It's a little something I was working on before we left Kittery. Its not perfect, but it's the best I've got." I announce. This wasn't true. I had been learning this song for one reason. Inspiration. She is my inspiration for everything these days. But letting everyone know this at this moment would be awkward and too real. So I lied. And I did it. With a smile. I place my hands upon the white and black keys and begin to play a soft, gentle F key melody. My fingers begin on the inside of the keys and trickle out towards the sides and tickle the black keys ever so gently creating a rain drop affect.

The sound was crisp and delicate. Before I realize it the notes are releasing from my mouth, like puffs of smoke in the air.

"A drop in the ocean,
A change in the weather.
I was praying that you and me might, end up together
It's like wishing for rain, as I stand in the desert.
But I'm holding you closer than most.
Cause you are my heaven. I don't wanna waste the weekend
If you don't love me, pretend a few more hours, then it's time to go.
As my train rolls down the east coast. I wonder how you keep warm It's too late to cry. I'm to broken to move on And still I can't let you be Most nights I hardly sleep
Don't take what you don't need from me.It's just a drop in the ocean,a change in the weather

Refuse to Sink

I was praying that you and me might, end up together."

I realize by the time the song is through that I had had my eyes closed the entire song. Maybe it was stage fright, or maybe I just let my fingers do the work. For whatever reason, when I opened them. I only saw Grace. My mother was gone, my brother and Aria where weirdly absent as well. Grace Anne stood alone in my tunnel vision, clapping her hands.

As she walks towards me, the light rises behind her and my little family reemerged, clapping and shouting in pleasure. "For God's sake Anchor! I never knew you could do anything like that! Amazing!" Grace Anne shouts as she hugs my neck.
"That's my boy!" My mother says proudly.
"Holy crap!" Aria chimed in. Chance rolls is his eyes and says. "Wow Anch, you are so cool, not gay at all.." Aria laughs, as Chance is swatted by my mother.

Grace finds a seat on my lap and begins to peck at the keys, trying to make her own melody. I wallowed in this happy moment that sprung from yet another tragedy. If this was all I could get, then I'll take it. We all sat around the table enjoying my mother's precious gift. Grace Anne got to experience what made me so gitty waking through the door. She praised my mother on a job well done and admitted defeat to the strudel. It was only a matter of time.

My mother adores Grace and her sister Aria I can tell. She doesn't squint at her like she used to do to my other girlfriends. Or ask them what religion they worshiped, in hopes to see what kind of morals they possessed. One girl bless her heart, I had brought home and fully enjoyed in *that* way from time to time. Was nearly ran out of the house, when my mother caught wind that she was.... Gasp..... Atheist. My mother shrieked at her. "You probably can't even spell Atheist! Go on. Sound it out. Oh Anchor you fool! I bet she can't spell class or bra either!"

Oh mom. She is such a hoot. Too bad. I really enjoyed her lack of a god. It never kept her from screaming to him though. Wink.

64

D. C. Garriott

Chapter Eleven

The next day, the social worker appears on the front steps of our home before the crack of dawn. And in one quick swoop, packs up all of Aria's things and carts her off to the neighboring town, to stay with her Aunt Jean. Who has two other children and a big enough heart to take in one more. See Mr. Keats sister, had expected Aria's arrival for a year now. She has known about the troublesome life the two girls had been living. She even offered to let Grace Anne come and finish school as well and attend a college close to them. Of course, Grace Anne already knew where she was meant to be. Even if that meant she'd have to sleep at friends houses until the blessed day when she graduated. Then she would be off to her new big life in the city.

Aria didn't shout or scream for Grace Anne. She calmly kissed her loving sister goodbye, as if they had expected this and planned accordingly. Tears were not shed only "I'll see you laters. " I am a little disarmed by the level of adulthood each of these miniature ladies exude. I envy their casual, carefree attitudes. After the goodbye Aria loads into the back of the van. The social worker turns to Grace Anne and I. "You ought to get a better job or go to school and live in a dorm because The Bank, will be taking the house at the end of the month, you have till then to get it together." she explains sharply without blinking. There is no denying the level of dope ass bitch, this lady was on. She had her own platform. And just like that. Grace Anne lost her father, her sister and her mother. All she had left was me.

Its been five days since the social worker took Aria away. Grace Anne has called her a few times, made small talk, just to see how her spirits are. I believe Grace misses her more than she knows. As expected, Aria is fine. She is adjusting well, she likes the home she knows it well

Refuse to Sink

from all their childhood visits. And is having fun with her cousins.

Grace Anne's father returned to the house, only to grab his possessions and to tell Grace Anne where he will be living. He found an apartment on the other side of town. He offered her the couch and wished her a belated birthday, which was weeks ago. He was clearly on his way to the liquor store. I decide to take Grace Anne out to dinner, to take her mind off the resent sadness and to have time alone with her again. Grace had just had a birthday, so I thought what better way to get her mind off the loss of her sister than a celebration.

We finish packing up her room across the way from my house. Going through old pictures, laughing and she reminisced the time she fell and chipped her tooth on the side of her bed. She's clumsy. Quirk #1 Now we are getting somewhere. Grace Anne gracefully slides the last of her totes from her room onto the bed of my truck. I follow with the huge collage she had made her freshman year of New York, depicting her dream and how she would accomplish it. Grace grabs the board away from me with a silly grin. She places a picture of us lying under my old tree in the backyard, she places it in the middle of the board.

"I have been waiting for my missing puzzle piece." I gasp and grab her waist, pulling her into my belt buckle, causing her to flinch. I release her and she pulls back grabbing the buttons of my shirt forcefully. Wow she means business. She pulls up on her tippy toes and touches her lips to mine and blows a puff of air into my mouth playfully. I stammer back while she jumps around laughing in complete humor of her actions.

"Damn it Gracie! Not cool!" I exclaim wiping the spit off my upper lip. Smiling, because there was nothing left to do. Seeing her like this was priceless. I will remember it, forever.

"Let's go Anchor. I'm starved half to death. I am sorry for my actions due to hunger!" She says while still giggling uncontrollably.

"Okay! You are are forgiven. Besides your spit taste like flower pollen. And I have become quite accustom to the smell of flowers." I profess.

"Oh Anchor. I think you are suffering from hunger pains as well!"

On the way to the restaurant. Grace Anne jokingly refers to me as an old man. I counter with a clucking noise. Insinuating, that she is a young chicken. This has a us giggling, yet again. I will be turning twenty soon and I suppose she thinks I am old. Yet neither one of us is old enough to be drunk, legally. I can only imagine what she would be like in this fashion(drunk). Probably slurring about plants and John Mayor. She swears on everything daily, that music helps plants grow. And that if music was on loud speaker, the world would be overcome by greenery.

"John Mayor, He's so calming, you sound a little like him when you sing" she says with a hint of fandom.

"Now I don't know about that, but okay." I laugh. She is just being nice.

We arrive at Casa De Something, the only Mexican restaurant in the whole town. Well Mexican/American. If you want authentic Mexican food, go to Mexico. After all, any place that claims to be legit yet has hamburgers on the menu, isn't authentic. Grace was always aggravated that it was the only restaurant, that served burritos. Since she was half Colombian, I guess she had every right. As we sit down at the table. Grace Anne speaks first.

"So about NYC...." she pauses to take a drink of her soda. "What's the chances of you joining me?" I knew this would happen. I knew I would have to choose. A cast of darkness covers my face. And she notices it immediately. She curls her lips to a precious pout. Her hands come together in prayer, she pleads. "Please Anchor. You make my heart thump and my days funny. I don't know how I will ever live without you!" she exclaims with too much dramatics.

"I'm sure you will find someone else to make you laugh and your girly parts tingle." I whisper hoping this is not true.

"You are disgusting. And No. I will never!" She shouts at me.

"Gah. Grace tell the world would you! Hush! Pipe down!" I shush her. She taps the side of her glass. Before I know it she has climbed on top of her stool and exclaims. "Can I have everybody's attention please?. Excuse me! Please." She waits.

"I would like to share it with the restaurant, that I indeed can not live without, Anchor Alcott Aldwin! And I would love it if you would clap if you agree, that he should run away with me!" The entire crowded restaurant, burst into over the top clapping. She slides down next to me

Refuse to Sink

and plants a tender, wet kiss on the side of my mouth. I reply " How can I argue with that??...." and stop shortly.

"With what?" she ask. "With that...." I point to her lips.

"So you'll go with this" she points to her face.

"No, that." I point back to her plump mouth.

"Oh you are gonna get plenty of that! Yay!" she proceeds to throw her arms around my neck in triumph.

"Yes Grace Anne, Lets Go To The City and Fall in Love" I rend the air. She takes a sip of her soda. "I knew you would see it my way" she smiles calmly.

After the dinner and I drop Grace Anne back off at her, soon to be possessed by the bank house. I start to wonder, how this will work? What to tell my mother. She will be mortified. But Grace Anne has no one to answer to when she graduates in two days, then she is free. I want to be free too. I find my inner Anchor becoming envious of her, then quickly dismiss it. Only for it to reappear seconds later. Her soul is free. She is almost unaffected by her parents actions and all her responsibilities. She looks ahead with hope and is fearless. I used to be like that. I used to dream of going to college, learning something brilliant that I can share with the world. Piano, song writing. Something like that. Maybe even a book one day.

Before my life came crashing down and I didn't know whether to run away or stand up and take my fathers place, which I could never do. I'm not him and would never be cut out to do as he has done. My mother depends on me. At least I think so. Or is that my conscience trying to rid me of this crazy idea. That I might follow her. How could I not follow her? She is the only glue that holds me. She binds me. She opens my heart, letting so much light in. Light I desperately need. How in the world could I deny my soul that?

I walk in my front door and sit down next to my mother on the couch its late so she has fallen asleep with her book on her chest. I slide in beside her and lift the book off, she starts. "Anchor? What time is it?" she says sleepily. "Its midnight." I disclose. "I better get to bed, probably been here for hours. How was your date?" she inquires.

"It was great, fine, good." I say nervously.

"Why are you babbling, what is it Anchor. Your hiding something" she looks at me trying to seek out my lies.

"Its nothing.. " I pause

D. C. Garriott

"Its something" she assures me.

"Grace wants to move to New York" I blurt it out so fast I couldn't retract it or sugar coat it, even if I erased her memory. "She What?!" shouting now. "And you? What do you have to do with this?" Wishing I had one of those little mind erasing pens from Men in Black. I now regret saying, everything I have just said. I look up at her with the best puppy dog eyes I can muster. Hoping this sways her just a little.

" I want to go with her." I wince awaiting her reaction.

Her book slams to the floor, she walks calmly down to her room and shuts the door. I am left in silence. This did not go well. I estimate to myself. My breath seems heavier than normal. Like I had just been kicked in the stomach. I dread the morning, my mother is not one to stop a conversation mid boil. She is hurt. I've hurt my mother. My heart sinks. I surely don't look forward to the morning. I know what it will bring. More hurt to the only woman I have ever loved truly.

I was right I had gotten four hours of sleep, on account of the tossing and turning. I thought about what it would be like to wave goodbye to Grace. And then what it would feel like to wave goodbye to my mother and Chance. Each seemingly as hurtful as the other. My dreams are filled with conflicting emotions, sadness, excitement and a constant woe of Grace Anne. She can be quite powerful, lingering around every corner to set a smile on my face from ear to ear.

When I awake I feel someone looking at me. I spin around across my bed, and there she is standing in my door way, with her arms crossed and a desperate look of confusion and pain on her face. "Mom I'm sorry I wont go. I - I'll just visit her from time to." She interrupts my pleading. "I am only going to say this once. I think it's a bad idea" She continues her speech. "But you are a man, with a future and who am I to say its not yours." I counter. "Really? But you need me here?"

"Not like you think I do Anch. I need you happy, and your brother happy and you're not going to be happy if I take this away from you. You have had enough taken away this year. GO." she demands. I have never loved my mother more. She was never over bearing and always respectful of my privacy, not like my friends mothers in high school. One day, I had went home with my friend Mattie and we found his mother, in his room under his bed searching, for whatever it was she had planned to bust him with that day. I always felt sorry for him. She made it impossible for him to do anything useful or fun. He is now in California attending college, as

69

Refuse to Sink

far away from his intruding mother as he can get. I think my mother just wanted to hold on to me, so she didn't push or pry she just as the Beatles would say "Let it Be". I am sure that's why our relationship has stayed somewhat cordial throughout the years of my breaking curfew and chasing girls. My mother grew up with all brothers. So I am sure she had an idea of what I was doing and how I would feel if she ever let on that she knew. So when she finally agreed to let me be. I wasn't surprised but I could sense the hurt and that it would eventually fade. Or maybe not, all I know is she is not holding me back.

Grace Anne's graduation day is today. She comes running across the lengthy yard between her house and mine and bounces into my arms so hard that it almost throws me to the ground.

"Do I look like a dunce? Tell me… I think so." she shakes her hair back away from her face. She is covered from head to toes in black and yellow there are some ribbons and medals around her neck that I take it are scholar awards. Of course. She shines and as always, looks perfect.

"You look amazing, smart, and older. Amazing Gracie." I reply with a smirk. Very impressed by my witty pun.

Her eyes squint, like she is trying to persuade me to see it her way. With no luck, she reaches up and grabs my face and plants a wet kiss on my lips, that lingered even after she pranced away. My mother and brother usher out of the house dressed in their Sunday best and wave me over. I look back and see Grace Anne and her mother getting into their Coal gray van, and head off for the school auditorium.

My family proudly packs into my mother's station wagon and we follow behind them. I see Aria waving at us from the back seat. This is the first time I have seen her since she moved away. She seems in high spirits. My mother makes a snide comment about Flora.

"Don't know how she shows her face on this blessed day." This shocks me a bit since my mother usually never talks behind any ones back.

"Well it is her daughters graduation, maybe she is here to take the credit she doesn't deserve?" I answer.

As we take our seats on the bleachers and settle in for the one hundred graduation student roll call. I see Grace standing up in the mist of all the black and gold. Smiling and waving. Blowing kisses, chatting with the friends she will probably never see again. I know a little bit about graduation, since I just went through it. Except I had my mother father and little brother there and they actually *wanted* to be there. Not

70

D. C. Garriott

expecting any type of acknowledgments like *her* mother.

I recall seeing Grace Anne smile at her mother, once. I know she loves her and respects her in some way, but she is damaged by her and begs not to become her. Never the less I hope she is at least thankful that she is here and her sister is here, to see her succeed. I follow her eyes to the side of the bleachers to where she is fixated now. I notice her father standing in the crowd. He is dressed in black and looks to have cleaned up for the ceremony. He looks nice. I see Grace wave that half wave she waved to me the first day I met her. She looks up at me with a look of confusion and courage. Her eye brows curl to the center of her face, then relax.

Finally the graduation begins. They begin to call out names, each person given a piece of paper with their credentials on it and a shake of the hand. GRACE ANNE KEATS. She raises up to a roar of the crowd and walks effortlessly to the stage. Valedictorian of the Class of 2010. She courtesy's and receives her paper and more metals than she can hold in one hand. She heads to the podium pushes her heavy black hair away from her face. Looking out over the crowd she begins to speak.

"Hello to all my education companions! I am thankful for the honor of being your Valedictorian! Our schooling may be over, yet it may continue on in some of our lives. Education will continue in everything you choose to do from here. Just remember the good times and the memories, the rest will come as life intends it so. A wise man once said. A graduation ceremony is an event where the commencement speaker tells thousands of students dressed in identical caps and gowns, that "Individuality" is the key to success. Well I agree! So throw off those caps and claim your identity and your individuality!!!! We are set free to sail and discover all the world has to offer."

She reaches to her cap and tosses it into the air, as the rest of the graduates do. Then she looks at me. We get lost in this perfect moment. I think that last line was not intended to give confidence to her fellow graduates, but to me. To reassure me that this is a good decision. Maybe I put off a vibe of fright or nervousness, with good reason. But I have to step it up, be the man she wants me to be, or it all will become unworth it to her eventually. That will be the day I lose the beating in my chest, that makes this all worth it.

We spend the next few days getting ready for our ten hour train ride.

Refuse to Sink

I hand over the keys to my truck to my mother since we will be in a five story walk up in the city. I will have no place for it. She accepts and grabs me around my neck holding on for dear life. I assure her that I will be back soon, and how a phone works both ways. I never want to end up mechanical with my mother, like she is with hers. Grace Anne spends a whole day going around, saying "Goodbye" to friends and family. She makes it a point to tell each and every one of them, how important they were to her to keep them in her back pocket, as she does everyone she meets. Her personality just does that. I think its called an "Addictive personality". If so, that's what she is. I spend the day on the beach with my little brother. He is taking the news quite well, for someone who is still mourning his father. I assure him that the returning school year will be full of changes. In his body and his mind. He will grow over the summer into a different person. He winces at the thought of me saying the word puberty. So I omit that word. "I am one phone call way little brother. I can hear you in the city. I just can't see you." Tears well up in my eyes. I try to hide my affection.

"Anchor?" said with trembling emotion. "Will I miss you like I miss dad?" He lays his head on my shoulder.

"I don't think so little brother. I am not gone. I am just away. Just pick up the phone and dial if you miss me. I will always answer." I reply, trying to keep my voice from cracking. "I love you Anchor. I miss you already. Do you miss me?" Chance says with a bright smile.

My face calms and a smile reemerges. "Yes my dear foe. I miss you so much I can't leave without doing one thing." Smacking the back of his head so hard it knocks his hat off. He retaliates, shoving my back to the ground. We wrestle there for a while, then we pick up our things and head to dinner with mom. The table is warm, we all set around it talking about my up coming trip. My mother packs up a big baskets of my strudels and pats Grace on the shoulder. "You take care of my boy."

"You have my word, Wynna." She responds with certainty.

D. C. Garriott

Chapter Twelve

Grace Anne and I sit outside the train station on a wooden bench. The weather is perfect, you can smell the flowers and feel the bright sun turning your skin to a different shade, right in front of your eyes. We await the train that will undeniably take us on our first unforgettable journey. I do not feel fear anymore, just a sense of being home. I am home in her eyes, where ever they are is where I belong. And if they are destined for the city, then so am I. Grace Anne has the phone to her ear. I hear Aria on the other line telling her to be careful and have fun and I feel a tap on my shoulder.

I turn around and my father stands with a smile on his face. "Hello Father." I say without the slightest hint of confusion as to why he is there. My mother and brother creep out from behind him, as if they were molded into him. They all stare at me with black unfocused eyes. My mother reaches out for me, only to be held back by my fathers huge wing - like arm. They are under him. Unable to be released. Why does he have them trapped? And I am free? My confusion builds. Grace Anne turns to me on the bench, her eyes burn black. I can see my reflection. I look closer into her mirror eyes, to find a bullet hole to my forehead. The blood drips down to my nose then to my lips. I grab my face and stare at my hands. No blood. "STOP IT DAD! NOW let me go!" I shout. He begins to fade. Grace becomes a blur. She is fading into a white airy space. "Grace! Stop! I'm coming!" I take off for her. Running, becoming short of breath quickly. My feet hit the pavement so hard I look down to see what I'm splashing through, its blood. I try to refocus my sight. I realize I am covered. Blood, there is so much blood. I glance at the pavement and see fliers and books thrown about. Where am I? The pain in my temples begins to fade. I stop and steady myself. Looking around

Refuse to Sink

my feet are planted, yet the pictures are floating around me, as if they are in a globe. I am in a snow globe.

What the hell is going on? The snow begins to fall around me. NYC Welcome Fall students. The fliers are swirling around my face. My body spins with the fliers. I try to make sense of the globe. When I look up I see my father wink at me. Through the line ceiling. Then he sets the snow globe down on the table next to his beloved arm chair, in the house that I grew up in. I am brought back to life by a voice. "Anchor? Wake Up!" I start.

"You feel asleep Anch." she says quietly.

"Good thing we have a private suite. Or you would've interrupted everybody's quiet!" she exclaims.

"Ha! Really! Damn I'm sorry." Shaking off the mid-day dream.

I am pretty sure it was Shakespeare that said. "Dreams are the children of an idle brain." I guess that makes sense. Then what would nightmares be? Wiping away the thought. I grab her inner thigh, in hints that I want to fool around.

Anything to erase what I had just experienced. What was that all about? Why the blood, the fading people? Why did their eyes look like that? Why was I on a NYC campus? Weird. She wipes my hand away, as quickly as I sat it there. "Anch! Really? You haven't had your eyes open two minutes!" she snaps with a lop-sided smile.

I reach up and grab her sweet, soft face. In the small cabin, that wasn't big enough to swing at a cat. She tumbles down onto my chest, tickling my torso with kisses, that set my whole body on fire. She is humoring me. Knowing that she has made me wait to touch her in that way. Its like waiting for a Christmas that never comes. My body cant help but project. It is being robbed of pleasure. She gazes up at me and her eyes twinkle against the sun. Wow. I am the luckiest man alive.

"New York City, land of the flies, trash and bad manners." I say with affliction.

"Anchor, you have never been there, you are basing your opinions from T.V and movies." she bats back.

"Nope, just word of mouth, my lovely." trying to diffuse her growing annoyance with me.

"It will be beautiful, and fun, and magical." she says staring out the train window. "Yes, it will be. Because it is gaining you." I say cheaply.

"The apartment is on the lower east side, its already beautiful there."

D. C. Garriott

Grace Anne smiles in defeat.

I spend a lot of time holding her. Thinking, this is just where I am meant to be. Beside her. This girl. My future. "No matter what you think about the city Grace. I know its dangerous and am determined to keep you safe." I announce.

"Anchor walking into a light post is dangerous, but you made it through alright." she snickers. I laugh and grimace as I remember the pain to my face.

I begin to hum a tune I had been tinkering with the last couple of weeks. And she drifts off to sleep, with her head in my lap. I stroke her long black hair, I watch her breathe, and her eyes flicker in dreamland.

Grace Anne and I arrive in the big city. Walking up the floors to our new nest. I feel my chest begin to pump. Her face is aflame with pleasure. There's a lot of steps. Finally and out of breath, we set our bags down onto the small furnished studio apartment floor, that is in desperate need of spring cleaning. It is as wide open as wide open gets. No walls to connect a room to, except for the extremely small bathroom,that attaches to the even smaller kitchen.

I exhale. Its like walking into a big bedroom/cell. The mattress lies in the middle of the room. A simple couch and a bulky, brown coffee table rest in the corner by the bar, that extends out from the tiny box of a kitchen. The kitchen only holds a stove, sink and I think that's a dishwasher? I sure hope so. I smell mold, and get a chill of left over spirits. The dust has settled and poufs up at the contact of our luggage. I let out a dangerous sneeze. Grace Anne grabs a mop with a smile and some cleaning supplies and begins to scrub. While I watch her. I fancy how happy she is and that I have made this happen. Even though she would've come without me. Or would she. And even if she did, would she be this happy? Who am I kidding, all boasting aside she made this happen. For both of us.

"What do you like most about the place Grace? The tiny ass- pot or the big ass window that we will never be able to cover with curtains?" I ask with a smile.

"I like it all, I take that back, I don't like the tiny "ass-pot" Because I don't know what that is. Also I don't how I'm going to Windex that window!" she glares at me.

"Ha!" I laugh because after all who really calls a toilet that anyway.

Refuse to Sink

After the clean-up and we have everything in its place, she and I sit down in front of the glass window that stretches from the floor and ends at the ceiling. We watch the sun set over the city. While we eat our ordered in Chinese food.

"Its not okay to fall in Love, you know?" Breaking the silence. She questions. "Well why not Anchor? Everybody does it eventually."

"Falling in Love is a mistake greater than any mistake you can ever make because you loose yourself to the other person, and you never get it back." I softly reply.

"I'll give you back, I promise" she returns.

"Gracie, you have had me in your back pocket, since the first minute I saw your face nothing could ever pull me away from those eyes those lips.." I pause I feel my temperature begin to rise.

"So the mistake you made, was falling in love with me Anchor? " she says with a hint of sadness. She wraps her arms around her chest in comfort. She couldn't possibly believe that I would regret anything about her.

"Yes my dear, the greatest mistake I have ever made. I Love You Grace, more than I love myself, so you can have me. And keep me. I don't want it back, its yours forever." I exclaim tossing a noodle in the air.

"I love you too, Anchor and I don't think Love is a mistake. I think it is a blessing, something that is given to you. You were given to me Anchor and I will keep you. She says with power in her eyes.

I grab her around the waist, laying her down on the uncovered mattress. She grabs my button down shirt with force, as she has done before. This time, she lightly unbuttons all the buttons one by one. Exposing my chest. She dances her tender fingers, down to my belt buckle and begins to undo the strap. My zipper is undone, its my turn to help her out of her clothes. Her arms raise high above her head turning her body into some form of ballet pose. Her back is tilted; I run my hands over her straps and pluck them open, her enclosed breast fall to their natural form. I lick my lips, to remove the spit the panting has caused. She leans up with her elongated back and presses her lips to mine in the most perfect way. I begin to make love to the girl; I just for the first time declared and felt that I truly did LOVE with all my heart. We join together like puzzle pieces, she is so soft and lovely and loves to be loved by me. Our bodies melt together, she flows so softly underneath my body.

The warmth runs throughout my skin, electrifying my fingertips, my breath is barley noticeable. It is so quiet. I massage her and remove any remaining clothing that hinders the moment. She is beautiful. She sparkles in the moon light and moans at all the right times. My mouth almost watering, my forehead full of tiny sweat beads. Her body floating in the midnight air. She is tender almost ghost-like. Yet, she is no ghost. I feel every inch of her magnificent elegance. We both have our moments. We find ourselves out of air, lying next to each other, basking in the exquisiteness of this first experience. And I thought the theater was astonishing. This was literally, breathtaking.

"This is what I have waited so long for?" she says with a smirk.

"No, this is what I've been waiting so long for." I state. She laughs and we hold each other tightly falling asleep in the bliss of bewilderment.

After our first time being together everything else seemed to fall into place. Our attitudes meshed better. I didn't have so much build up that I felt I might explode! We had such great lovers banter that I'm sure it could rival Lucy and Rickey's. How's the old saying go? "Two Peas in A Pod?" Yep. Just like that.

She's a mess of gorgeous and chaos, you can see the city in her eyes. I write in my journal while I watch her get ready for her first day at her new job. "She is right where she belongs not in the City but with me" I continue to write.

"Falling in Love with her was indeed my greatest mistake. Because I am down for the count."

She tosses her dark hair back. 5

She caresses her lips with gloss. 4

She does her "smile face" in the mirror. 3

She tucks her shirt into her pants. 2

She turns around and winks at me. 1

Before she knows it, the journal hit's the floor. I am around her waist with force. She yelps in laughter, as I toss her atop my shoulders and sling her down to the bed. "Anchor! I have to go to work!" she tries to let out through all the kisses being forced to her lips.

"I'm sorry, but you are so amazing, I cant stop what it does to me!" I say with full fluster.

"Well you and all That. She circles below my waist line. Will have to wait until four." she says pointing to her biggest fan located in my pants. She manages to remove herself from my embrace and heads to the door. I

Refuse to Sink

follow her, on my knees. Where I remain, until the door shuts behind her.

I haven't written in my journal, since the day my father died. I normally only write down things I don't want to forget in here. But my mother was adamant about me telling her everything that is going on with us, in the city. So I promised her I would take it along with me. Now it's coming in handy, because I don't want to forget the way she swings her hair around trying to get it to go into a perfect pony tail. The gentle rhythm she possesses when she walks, like a ballerina. The way her lips curl up when she reads. I always catch her trying to read my journal and I snatch it away as quick as she gets her hands on it. She could probably find something more interesting to read than my sloppy handwriting and bad spelling.

We have been in New York for three months, eighteen days and fifteen seconds. I know that, because I remember the exact moment of our first night together. Grace Anne has of course, nailed the job as grounds keeper at Central Park. She brings home stories of the lay of the land and beautiful flowers that she was given as extra to plant on our balcony, that is slowly running out of room. My allergies have kicked up but its all worth it. To watch her obsession unfold is entertaining, to say the least.

Grace Anne has to be at the Park at quarter till eight every morning and returns home around four thirty. So by the time I open my eyes she is already up and gone. I usually hear her get up and receive a soft kiss to my forehead as she exits. I woke up today to leave for my new job. That I received from one of my fathers partners, here in New York. Mr. Jones hired me as an assistant I believe out of sheer remorse for my loss and respect for my father. On any account; I agreed to work for him. I don't necessarily like my job, but I start late and get off early, so I don't complain.

I got accepted at NYC but my classes don't start until the Fall. If that's what my father was pointing to in that ghost induced nightmare on the train, then the point was well received. So in the meantime I pull my weight. During a short break from Mr. Jones Office. I stroll down one of the streets. I'm not even going to try and tell you if it was 8th or 18th street, because I never look at signs. I just go by places that are familiar and end up getting myself lost every time. My tactics from Kittery, just don't work here. Turning the corner I see a shop with twinkling lights

D. C. Garriott

and shiny things. I am enchanted. It drew me closer. I take a seat on the bench that sits directly in front of the grand window, eating a street bagel (That I said I'd never do) and admire the buildings beauty, not really looking at anything in particular. I glance down at the side walk, where something else has attracted my glance. Its like, it was begging for me to notice it. Its puffy yellow top, shot straight up out of he concrete. It was a dandelion and my father had put it there. *Hello Dad.* I thought to myself. Smiling I turn back to my previous attachment. There it sat. The most beautiful diamond I have ever seen. My first thought was not how much? Or what kind? I thought of Grace and how it still wasn't as beautiful as she.

I wondered if my father was nudging me forward. I walk somewhat against my will, into the store and catch eyes with the minuet man behind the counter that is almost as tall as he. I here elevator music and not surprising I like it. It reminds me of my mother. He smiles, as if he knows what I want. Of course he does, isn't this a jewelry store? I couldn't be here to buy cheese. The little Asian man addresses me. "Hello young man, can I help you find something?" "Actually, I am interested in the ring that's on display."
I say with some false confidence.
"Ahhh the Forever Diamond." he says with a little to much hope.
Why do they always have such catchy names for these rings? Like the name should sell it, even if the beauty doesn't?
"Yes that one. Could I bother you for a price?" I ask.
"That one sir, goes for five thousand." he answers.

My heart drops to the floor and shatters all hope of presenting my forever, with her forever. I look shocked and a little sad, when the old man says. "Have you ever financed anything?"
"Nope" I answer.
"Well lets see what we can do then" he leads me into a room that is small but hugely intimidating.

I come out a proud owner of the Forever Diamond and cannot wait a second, to place it on her hand. But I have to wait till the exact right moment, because up until this very moment. I have been a fool in her eyes. A backwards, nervous unconfident man that still gets tongue tied every so often around her! Deep concern sets in. Will she even say yes? Will she laugh and not take my words seriously? What am I doing? I place the box in the side pocket of my jacket walking back into my work

Refuse to Sink

building, with a hint of depression. And a bit of excitement, not to be over shadowed by doubt.

I try to act like I haven't, just made the biggest purchase of my life and that I will probably drown in the payments soon enough.

Grace Anne meets me at the steps of our humble apartment, with a sack full of burgers and a couple Cd's she picked up at the music store a couple blocks away. "What's up Chuck? I got you a C.D of piano music to help with those lyrics you've been writing." she says as she kisses my cheek and retrieves the mail from the small lock box. I wonder softly. What lyrics? And blush at the thought of her seeing my journal.

"Is that a letter from Aria?" I ask.

"You know it is. Every Friday, like clockwork. Probably telling me how much she hates her cousins, and how much she misses me." she says with a chuckle.

"Well she does. Chance called this morning apparently he is in trouble for something involving a stick and another kids eye." I assure her that the kid didn't lose the eye. "And have you been nosing in my Journal again Grace?" I ask her, following her up the stairs.

"No Anchor, gah. Yes.. Yes I have. Don't be mad." she stuttered.

"I'm not mad, but we will definitely have make-up sex later, just for good measure." I say slyly with a wink and a smack to her bottom. That causes her to almost lose our brown bag dinners, down the steps.

D. C. Garriott

Chapter Thirteen

It is Christmas Day. Grace and I exchange gifts, under our little Charlie Brown tree (as Grace lovingly refers to it.) Its little. But Grace grew it. And decorated it. And that makes it the most special tree in the world. She bought me a pair of Ray Ban sun glasses, that I will never wear. Ever. A pack of socks, that I'm sure was a joke. I have a feeling, she has no clue how to give a gift. I give her a porcelain figurine of lady liberty, the same one my father bought my mother, on his last visit home. I didn't have to look very hard for it, since they sell them on every street corner in this city. I could almost feel him smiling down on me, with pride.

She loved it also she loved the eighteen other presents I showered her with. It was the first time I had been able to buy her anything, so it got a little out of hand. It was worth it because I got a smile and a kiss after every single one that she opened. Calls to the parents were made and she spoke to her sister and promised a visit in the next few months. After all the catching up on the phone and listening to the hyped up siblings, tell us in detail everything about their experiences with Santa Clause. We found quiet in our little life together. She pulled cookies from the oven, as I set behind my keyboard playing her new chords that I had been learning recently and a couple Christmas songs that I knew.

"Anch? What do you think about babies?" she asked over the sound of the keyboard.

"I don't" Taking my eyes away from the notes long enough to smile.

"No really, would you ever want one? Like years from now. I know I'm only eighteen so its not an option." she says sternly.

"Well its an option. Haven't you ever seen those reality shows, with all

Refuse to Sink

those ugly girls getting pregnant? Then getting rich and fake boobs?" I say with a laugh. She smiles and responds.

"Did you just call me ugly?"

We both laugh at our foolish conversation, and settle in on our long dark green couch, in front of our never stopping city window. We begin to eat our microwave Christmas dinners. While watching the snow fall, so softly over our terrace. I thought about honoring this night, with the ring. But I withdrawal even though this moment is perfect, this is not our moment.

Throughout the next week I tried desperately to find the right moment. I thought about what I would say and how I would say it. If it was possible to pull this off without saying something incredibly stupid or immature. I bumble through each day, trying not to alert her or propose while she eats cereal. I have to do this soon. Or I might ruin it or loose the ring. But perfect is my only option. And perfect it will be. Dad. I need your help.

New Years Eve lights, fall over the city. Excited people flood the streets. They wear lights around their necks and seem to be in herds. Grace and I make our way through the crowds to a upper east side party thrown by her "Park" people. Grace Anne is dressed to the max with a short sparkling gray mini dress, her hair is up in an Egyptian bun. She looks stunning, with her heels high and her make-up shimmering in the Christmas lights. She had rented me a tux, even though I opted out of the jacket and just donned the gray vest and slacks. I looked hot. She looked gorgeous. This is our night, this is our time.

I lose her on purpose when we enter the party, claiming I had to use the "Ass-pot." One of her friends, that was in cahoots with me lead her out to the lower terrace. Above that terrace, lye a balcony surrounded by white twinkling Christmas lights. In the middle, sat a white Baby Grand. That was strategically placed there, before the event. I took my place behind it and begin to play a soft, silky melody. She looks up ward towards me. Her attention is drawn. I bite the bullet and begin to sing.

Forever can never be long enough for me
Feel like I've had long enough with you,
Forget the world now we won't let them see
But there's one thing left to do.
Now that the weight has lifted Love has surely shifted my way.
Marry Me?

D. C. Garriott

Today and every day
Marry Me? Say you will.

By the time I am finished with my song. The whole party has grown silent. People have flooded out to the lower terrace, surrounding her grabbing their mouths in I hope. Happiness. But It could be shock, towards my sad attempt at romance. I was being a modern day Romeo dammit!

She stands below me with her mouth wide open, a single tear rest on her blushed cheek. I rush down the spiral stair case finding myself out of breath, standing in front of a finally, flabbergasted Grace Anne.
"Based on Psycho logic Study, a crush only last for a maximum of four months. If it exceeds, then you are already in Love" She looks at me with a sparkle in her eyes, accompanied by a crooked grin. I think, how perfect. This sets my next line up perfectly. "I fell in love with a sparkle of light. I fell in love with a halo. I fell in love, against my will. You were my light Grace, when I had none. If in the end I have learned nothing at all. I have learned, how to love you." I bend down, resting traditionally on one knee.
"Will you marry me Grace Anne Keats?"
She stands for a while stunned. Then she bends down to where I rest on my knee and softly says. "So I can keep you? " she smiles warmly and I nod yes.

She pulls me up and off bended knee into an embrace. I know now that she is mine forever. My face has never been so alive the smiles are real they project my heart. It is full and ready.

Now I walk the dirty streets of New York, as if they were the clean streets of Caribou. Waving foolishly at strangers, when normally I would be fully aware of what they are capable of. Nothing seemed to matter much after she said Yes. Not my awful job, that now I went to everyday with a smile on my face. My fathers absence, seemed to hurt a little less and the air in this nasty city, had become clean.

Grace Anne, being Grace Anne has already been going through wedding plans down to the last detail. Our wedding song the flowers (of course) even the guest list is a science. I can't understand the way a woman's mind works when they lock into something they want. But its her wedding and I intend to let her make the best of it. After all it was

Refuse to Sink

my big idea in the first place. The two of us sit across from one another at a small cafe, outside of Central Park. She is nose deep in a notebook, scribbling down things she has to get together before Friday. I just watch her. As she scratches her forehead with the pen, she glances up at me ever so often. To see if I am still concentrated on the task at hand. "What about Paris? Grace Anne asks me.

"Grace you know we cant afford Paris! And Really? What an overstated place to go! " I say with a laugh.

"Its the City Of Love Anch!!!!!!!!! How can you overstate that?" she shouts. I take a bite of my sandwich that is surely far more interesting than Paris.

"On the contrary my dear, it is the City of Lights." I respond expertly. "Well I think its romantic, decadent & fascinating." she says with a smile. " Of course you do." I laugh.

"Really Anch, you wont even consider? Did you know that Paris is considered one of the greenest and most livable cities in Europe?" she attempts to educate me.

"Now who has all the useless information. It is also the most expensive!" I challenge her.

"Anch!!" she shouts at me losing her will too fight. She scoots her heavy iron cafe chair closer to me making a screeching noise, that seems to interrupt everyone on the patios lunch. She runs her small index finger across my lips.

"I think you want to go with me. You just love to argue with me." She passes a seductive kiss across my neck line.

My insides go crazy and I'm left feeling defeated by her sexual power over me. "You know Jim Morrison's grave is there? Maybe we would go see it. I know you love him." Rolling her eyes.

"Ah you mock me! I don't love him. I respect him. Also I believe that Henry Miller, in the book Tropic of Cancer said "Paris was like a beautiful prostitute in the distant evening light. The closer one gets, the more is revealed. The imperfections become more apparent," Err... something of that nature." She kisses me again. And bats her beautiful hazel eyes. "It is full of people that sleep all afternoon and hate us for being there. Also I'm pretty sure people pee in the streets. They make New York City, look good." I exclaim, fighting against her caresses.

Grace Anne laughs and continues. "Impressive." she says with confidence. "I will go there one day and you will be by my side. Pointing

out all the flaws, making jokes about the statues and the locals. Loathing the whole experience. I cant wait to see it!" I reply.
"Grace you are right about that! But I couldn't hate the City of Love because I would be able to see you smile; I would find the beauty in that place. Just like I found the beauty of New York." She tosses her hair back and smiles.

We have been making plans for the wedding and honey moon for weeks and planning a trip home to boot! I am stressed with payments on the ring and the wedding. The Park allowed Grace Anne to make reservations for our wedding there, for free. So that's one weight off my shoulders, the quest list isn't too long so that helps too. But all these bills are coming in from cake makers and flower people talking in a languages I don't understand. So I construct a well written note everyday, leaving it for Grace when she gets home. She can take care of returning the phone calls.

I want to take her to Paris. So I am. I called a few of my dads old work buddies and they, by the grace of God. Secured us plane tickets and a hotel. With all their kindness I have few words but, "Thank you" to give them. They are tucked safely in my journal. She wont know until the day of the wedding. She thinks we will do something like a cottage in the Hampton's or a trip back to her hometown, to combine the two trips we had planned. It will make her whole year and surely will be a priceless moment, for both of us. She returns home, with a huge bouquet of flowers hiding her face. She lays the flowers softly on the counter and finds me in mid thought. I smile, she questions.
"What Anch? Are you hiding something from me?" I laugh and say "Never my dear, never!" I kiss her pouting lips, she believes me. It was the first time I actually lied to her face. But it was worth it.

The big day arrives and I feel a sense of relief seeing my mother rustling through a bag, looking for my brothers cufflinks.
"Where the hell are they!" she shouts. Its so stuffy in this small dressing room and her angry painting, is making the steam thicker.
The families had flown in from Caribou two days prior to the wedding. To throw Grace Anne a bridal party, have the rehearsal dinner and such. I accept her help as well as Flora's even though I can barely stand to have her within fifteen feet of me. Since the awfulness of Caribou that blessed night, she has been a little more involved in Gracie's life. Maybe its because she doesn't really have to take care of her anymore? She is no

Refuse to Sink

longer a burden.

On any account, Grace seems to be glad she is here, as well as my mother, who she has gotten very close to over the past year. My mother refers to her as"The daughter, she never thought she'd have." This is of course the nicest thing my mother has said to her, since she found out about the wedding.

"Mother! Language please!" I shout at her with a hint of laughter.

"There is probably a pastor around here somewhere." She chuckles, throwing her hand over her mouth. Chance walks up to her, handing her a handful of shining cufflinks. "Mine and Anchor's Momma." he says slyly. "Are you trying to give me a heart attack? Anchor you have ten minutes, then its show time. Are you ready for this?" She says, retract fully.

I smile. "As ready as I'll ever be Momma. Go check on Grace Anne. Leave Chance. We need to go over his toast." My mother heads out in haste. Swinging her dress behind her. I am enjoying my mother today. She is fresh and bright and no longer dragging around, as if she's lost her puppy. She has changed. Chance has changed. What a difference time makes.

"I assume she looks beautiful." Chance says with envy. Rolling his eyes he continues. "What do you think Dad would say, if he were here?"

"I don't know brother, maybe a "Go get um boy?" I respond bitterly.

"I think he would tell you your crazy. And you wouldn't listen. That's how it would go down." he snaps.

"Do you think I'm crazy Chance?" I ask.

"I know you are crazy Anchor. But I also know you love that girl. Even though, I don't see what all the fuss is about." he says with a hint of disgust.

"Oh little brother. You slay me." I wink and begin to shove him out the door towards the alter entrance. "Just don't screw up, loser." I wink and wave him off.

★

D. C. Garriott

I walk out onto the silky walkway. Its so bright, all the white blares into my eyes. I look away to the trees that outline the aisle, shadowing the people placed in the white chairs. They all turn to look up at me. Some smile, some look away. Some I recognize, some I don't. Our family sides are pretty equal, an even twenty on both sides. Small, intimate. Exactly as Grace Anne saw it in her head, months before. Music begins to play as I reach the preacher, he shakes my hand. I smile at him nervously, then the music stops, then proceeds to gets louder. "Here comes the Bride" begins to play, the entire wedding party stands. My brother fidgets holding the rings. I glare at him. And move my lips, with no sound. Don't drop it.

She floats along the white pedaled path, like a spirit. Covered from head to toe, in ivory lace. Her veil hangs loosely across her face, her smile shines through clearly. As I knew it would. It takes a moment for her to reach where I am, so I bask in the glory of her undeniable beauty. Adorned in lace her beautiful, elegant gown flowed from under her breast, stretching at least a mile down the thin isle. The dress has a show stopping effect, the crowd of admirers gasp at her allure. The train a has a sparkle to it, like it is made with diamonds or glitter. I'm just glad other people are enjoying what I have seen all along; a princess, a trophy, a queen.

To bad it took dressing her for the part, for them to notice that she is indeed, dazzling. When she finally reaches me I proceed to pull the applique veil, from vaguely blocking my view. I notice her eyes are lightly covered in a pale pink shadow, kissed with mascara piercing through the lace finding the place in my heart, where they have always lived. The moment brings an unannounced tear to my eyes. The pastor speaks and goes about the process of the wedding. When he ask for our vows, she interrupts. "I know we did not plan on writing our own vows, but I want to say something to my Groom."

"I, Grace Anne take you, Anchor. To be my friend my lover, the father of my children and my husband. I will be yours in times of plenty and in times of want, in times of sickness and in times of health. In times of joy and in times of sorrow, in times of failure and in times of triumph. I promise to cherish and respect you, to care and protect you to comfort

Refuse to Sink

and encourage you and stay with you, for all eternity."

I am in shock ,just like the first day I met her. She really took time to think of this, or memorize it. This is just like her! I should have seen this coming! My feet lock and my mouth wont move. I blink. I am exasperated. Then I hear my father. I know exactly what he would say. "Snap out of it Boy! She had you at Hello!" No don't say that, she will turn and walk away, don't sell yourself short! Be brilliant! My conscious has developed into a full on shout now. Say something! I know exactly what to say to her. I hope it makes sense in words, as it does in my head.

"I've been beaten down. I've been kicked around,
But she takes it all for me.
And I lost my faith, in my darkest days.
But she makes me want to believe. They call her love.
She is love, and she is all I need."

Grace Anne smiles at my delivery. It was song like and brilliant. My inner Anchor is pleased. The pastor smiles and continues with. Repeat after me:

"This ring is a token of my love. I marry you with this ring, with all that I have and all that I am"
"I will forever wear this ring as a sign of my commitment and the desire of my heart"

We both say and repeat the words, with great emotion. We exchange our platinum rings. This is it she is mine! We turn as our new names our announced. The preacher announces. "Mr. and Mrs. Anchor Alcott!"

Everyone stands, roaring with delight. We walk hand in hand back down the isle. I catch glimpse of my mother and Flora. They both wear their gladness upon their faces with pride. We opt to toss dandelions and bird seed in honor of my father's hints thus far. My mother is of course all out bawling. She is so sweet. I don't think Flora can cry, since she is Satan. So she just comforts my wailing mother. I feel the bird seed smacking my brow. Grace Anne turns to me with a motherly smile reaches up patting the seed from my hair.

"Did we just do that?" her enchantment glowing.
"That we did my dear. That we did." my joy plastered all over my face.

D. C. Garriott

Chapter Fourteen

Walking through the park, where Grace Anne works. I hold a huge bouquet of flowers to surprise her. My new bride and I, have been living in a state of felicity since the wedding. My mother left and Flora disappeared yet again. To my excitement. I thought she might just move in, she was at our place for so long.

We are two days away from our trip. The trip to Paris, she still doesn't know about. I have managed to keep this from her all this time. I am overly proud of my self at the moment. Yet I am on my way to surprise her with a "flight" upstate, instead of train. She will never know what hit her when we reach the airport and board a flight to Paris. This feeling overwhelms my face. I feel a burn in my cheeks from my excessive smiling. My thoughts are carried away, when I render what it will be like, when we have our first son. Or daughter. What will they look like and how wonderful will Grace Anne be, as a mother? We have had the conversation about how long we will wait. She considers three years, because that will set her in the right position, to take time off from the park to spend with little Anchor Jr. "AJ". Grace Anne has already planned that name. For a boy or a girl. I told her that's unoriginal, she laughed at me with the reply. "Your name is original enough, for generations of Alcott's." Check and Mate.

Grace Anne sets alone at the long buffet table, in her dainty break room. She is early for work, awaiting her co workers. She hangs her head low, with worry. She should be pleasant and excited, because today is the day! Last day of work for two weeks, she gets to see her sister and spend some much needed time with her new husband.

"Hey Girl!" a coworker sets down next to Grace."Hey…. (gurgle)" Grace replies. With a conserved look the woman ask. "That didn't sound good

Refuse to Sink

girl.. Are you sick?"
"I am not feeling 100% today, maybe it's the weather or my allergies. Or the flu." she says running towards the restroom.
"Or your pregnant newly wed!" the co worker spats with laughter.
"NO way Laura! I have a five year plan! Grace Anne yells from the stall.
"Babies don't give a shit about your life plan. Ask one of my three sons."she responds, drinking her coffee.
When Grace Anne returns to the table smelling of eggs and greener than the park. She wipes her brow and replies. "Crap… What do I do?"
"You strap on your harness and get ready for the roller coaster ride of motherhood! Good luck sweetie. I'll see you when you get back. Now you take it easy on your trip okay?"she pats Grace on the back and heads out the swinging doors.

Grace Anne wipes the remainder of make up off her face and begins to smile, as she gazes at her reflection. *Could this be? Pregnant? I cant wait to tell Anchor. I wonder what he will say? Not in our Five Year Plan he will say. Mocking me. I know he will be supportive. I have never seen him be the latter. Today is going to be a good day. If this puking ever ceases.*

Strolling through the park without a hint of sadness, with nothing but good luck at my door. I am married to the most beautiful girl I have ever seen. And have made a life with her I never thought I would have, in a city he never thought I'd be in. And for all that I am proud of myself and feel so light on my feet. Like nothing in the world matters. My eyes go dark.

My left temple begins to throb. I try to blink, but it is not possible. I try to fight my way out of this reoccurring nightmare. I finally realize again, that this is not a dream. Its real. The air around me is black and through the darkness, in all the confusion; I drop the flowers. They fall to the ground. I can hear them smack the pavement, through the chaos I can hear someone talking.
"Wow dude.. first strike and he goes down" the second male shouts.
"I know right, I'm getting better" the first male exclaims with excitement.
"Hurry dude, come on" the second male says.

They begin fishing through my pockets, pulling out my wallet, opening it. The street thugs begin to pull out credit cards and money all the while a photo of Grace Anne floats in the air, then hits the pavement in front of me. The wind picks it up before I can grab it. It floats away.

90

D. C. Garriott

"I am shit, just wait, do you think he is dead??" the first male asked.

"Only one way to find out" the second male says. I begin to moan.. I see my father, through what seems like a long tunnel. His face is blurry and arms longer than they should be, reaching out towards mine. He moves closer to me. Somehow he has gotten so close, he is now laying next to me. His eyes shining and a cloud surrounds his body. The pavement shines underneath. "Hey boy." I hear him so clearly.
"This is not going to happen to you. Grab my hand and hold on tight." he winks at me.

A light around the crown of his head, is beaming and echoing. I see my life in flashes. My mother, Chance, my father, he is here. My ears ring and my throat goes dry. And last, Grace Anne. Her smile her heart glowing, "She dreams of castles in the sky." I hear myself say.

I look past my father into a corner of my mind, where she stands helpless. She is draped in satin, holding her belly with care. It has formed a slight bump. As she pats the bundle of love that rest on the inside. I wonder, if I'll ever get to do the same. Her eyes, they are bereaved. I've never seen her quite so broken. A light beams around her. I hear her say. "I'm sorry." I scream out to her, reaching upward. I grab her and she falls away from me, like sand through my fingers.

"Follow my light Anchor" she says as tears roll down her beautiful face and splash against the darkness, radiating and rippling, like ocean waves, across my eye lids. And I do. I let go. My body is sent swirling around in the universe. I ascend towards the clouds, spinning and turning violently. My father, follows me with a confident smile.

I awake in a puddle of sweat.

I grab at the sheet underneath me. A smell fills the air, that I know well. Its my mother strudel. Am I dead? Why do I smell my mothers cooking? Why am I in my old room? The sun hits my bedroom floor, like it has for the last 18 years. What the hell is going on?I repeat to myself. Raising up, shaking my pounding head back and fourth. Then I hear it. My fathers laugh. I spring out of bed, trampleing the dirty clothes leading to the hallway. Swinging around the staircase and tumbling down the steps. I follow the sound in a haze. When I pass the living room. I see

Refuse to Sink

Chance, happy, playing cars near the tall white fireplace. Jazz plays. This isn't right. I reach my mother, still wiping the sleep from my eyes.

"Your father just went outside to work on your brothers bike, you should go help." she says with a smile wider than ever. Flashes of my life thus far, cloud my confused mind. "He's where?" I stammer back.

"Outside Anchor. Go help. I'll make you breakfast." She says.

I feel sick to my stomach. Slowly I walk out to the shed. Like I am about to witness a paranormal act. There he is. I stand in the doorway stunned. My father stands up and says. "Dude, what happened to you? The sand man was not friendly to you!" he laughs to same Santa Claus laugh as before.

"Dad am I dreaming? Did I dream your death? Grace Anne? And Caribou?" my voice shakes.

"I don't think you slept last night boy. You look terrible, grab that wrench." he request.

"What the hell.No. Stop. Tell me what happened." I shout wiping sweat beads from my face.

"I suggest you watch your mouth. I have no idea what your talking about." he says sternly.

I cant breathe Grace fills my thoughts. My heart begins to hurt. Did I imagine her? Does she even exist? I have to know. I run back into the kitchen, sliding on the familiar rug that I have tripped over since I was a toddler. And realize, nothing has changed. Everything is in its place. My mother and brother are back to normal. Normal. What the hell? It was all so real. I have to find her. God dammit, will the dreams ever stop! Without complete thought. I began speaking in incomplete sentences. "Mom, I am going to go. On a trip. Today. Got to see, her. That place." my lips go numb.

"What? Where? Why?" she ask frightfully.

"I am almost twenty, I have a week off of work due to the Open. I'm headed out this afternoon!"she looks at me, puzzled.

"Okay?" she replies.

"No. You don't have the right to look at me in confusion!" I realize I am yelling at her.. I digress. "I'll be back soon, I love you." I recover.

I head towards the stairs, skimming over the family photos and knickknacks. While packing my bag. I grab my journal. When I open it, it begins the day my father died. But it wasn't about my father dieing. It was about him doing well, in New York and headed home today. I continue

92

D. C. Garriott

to shake my head, as if that, will turn this all around.

Even if I could, would I? Trade my fathers life, for a girl? Trade my mothers happiness, for my own? My brothers Santa Clause has returned. And I would never even think of putting him through that, again. What have I done? What has happened? The thoughts are manic and so am I.

I speed down the gravel road, glancing through the rear view at my new found normal life. I get a phone call. I automatically think. Its Grace Anne. When I look down, it is only my father. I find myself giddy with excitement at the fact that I can answer his phone calls, once again. So I do.

"Son? Where yah going?" he sounds concerned.

"Caribou. Dad." I answer.

"What's in Caribou son?

"I'm not sure, dad. But there is something I have to find. I'll call you if I find it." I say with a smile.

"Okay son. I don't know why you are on a treasure hunt, but okay. I'll be here when you get back. I have been permanently placed in Kittery, so no more long work weeks. Plan on retiring here in a couple years! What do you say about that!" he excitedly announces.

"I say. Its about time! I'll talk to you later Dad." I try to find my man voice. "I'll talk to you later." Wow. What a day. I have my dad back, my house my family. But that leaves Grace Anne. Where is she. Who is she? I will find her.

Speeding down the interstate, thinking of what I might say if I did find her, see her, talk to her. And before I know it. I am getting of the exit to Caribou. I follow the roads I know, to get back to my "Dream house" Crossing the train tracks. I realize that where my house once stood. Is a pasture. With a large black abandoned barn, leading out to a lake. This doesn't make sense. I regroup, staring at the abandoned property. I'll go to the movie theater. Is that real? Or another part of the dream? I guess I'm going to find out.

Driving down main street, the sun begins to set. I look out the window glancing at passer-buyers, thinking any one of them could be Grace Anne. But none were. The workers theater had never heard of her. I sit in my truck, head in my hands. It's over, she isn't here. She never existed. I have to be an adult and take a dream for what it is, a dream.

Refuse to Sink

When I return home, my mother hands me a handful of mail. While glancing through it I find a packet labeled. Admissions. NYC. "You weren't gone long." my father says to me in passing, holding a baseball glove and bat. "What I was looking for wasn't there." I answer back.
"Oh well if your looking for all your dirty clothes, they are now on the dryer. Pack them up to your room please." my mother interjects.

I grab my clothes off the dryer, carting them up to my room and place them in the chair. I plop down next to my keyboard. I begin to tap out the chords, of the very song I had written for Grace Anne. I am confused and very ill. I lay down on my twin bed, holding the letter from NYC to my chest. Then a thought comes to me. She could be there.

New York. I have to go there. Maybe I'll find her. I wont find anyone like her around here, that's for sure. I am not afraid anymore. I have nothing to fear really. My dad is fine. So am I. But Grace Anne is still out there. Waiting for me. I will find her. I drift off to sleep, just as I am drifting off. I am awakened by Chance, bouncing in and out of the doorway. "Get up, Anchor. Dinner."

I join my family in the dining room, still wiping the sleep from my eyes. My mother has made an enormous dinner, just as she always had. And my father had the newspaper plastered to his face, just as he always had.
"What was that pamphlet from NYC Anchor? My mother inquires. Passing my plate to me.
"It was my acceptance letter. I got into the music program." I look at my father for his expression. I am correct, his mouth is wide open.
"At a go BOY! When do you leave! Ahaha! NYC son! That's big!" He shouts.
"Can I have your room? I don't want to live in it, but I got tons of stuffys, that have been eying it for years." Chance looks at me with hopefulness.
"Calm Down Chance. Let him talk" said my mother, with excitement.
"I leave next month on the first. I'll take a train, since I know flights are expensive. I got enough left fo-r" My father interrupts me.
"Oh Son! Of course not! You are getting dropped off by your loving family! Looks like the whole Aldwin Family, is going to New York!" he exclaims, smiling like a fool. "I can finally take your mother to the Empire State Building, and Broadway!"he shouts, looking at my mother

who is beaming. "Wouldn't that be nice, Wynna?"

"Yes Alcott that would be amazing. I'm in. What about you Chance?" she points to my little brother.
"Anything to lose Anch. I'm in." He smiles wickedly in my direction.

I sit in silence. As if they gave a shit, if I wanted to go on a ten hour car trip with my mother blasting the saxophone C.D. Or my father telling City stories, we've all heard before. I sigh. And then there's Chance, with all his noises and questions. But you know what. I am looking forward to it. My heart swells double its size. My family. I love them.

Refuse to Sink

D. C. Garriott

Chapter Fifteen

The month passes without notice, it seems. I filled my time, tossing the baseball with Chance and helping my dad with everything from chores to model airplanes. But mostly; I searched for her. Her name. Her mothers name. Even her old addresses. Nothing. It came up other people. Not her. I had all but given up, by the day I was set to leave.

As I am loading the last piece of my life in Kittery, into my fathers brand new SUV. I believe he bought it, just for the trip. I'll never know I guess. Chance already has too much energy and my mother is packing tubs of Tupperware, full of my favorite blueberry crack.

"I think that's enough Wynna." my dad shouts from the car.

We all pile in and off we went. Throughout the ten hour trip. I heard stories about Nate King Cole, from my mother. President Reagan stories from my father. And the complete history of the tire swing, from my brother. We stopped at every little sweet shop and historical site. We ate at any "Authentic" diner, my father thought he might run into a celebrity at. It seemed never ending. But it was.

We pulled up to the front of NYC. My eyes widened and my heart sank. What if she's not here? I shake the thought. Ether way. I will fulfill my dream. I had to. I had to let her go. Or the thought of her, the dream. I had to let it all go. After a day of sight seeing my father, mother and Chance decide to head back to Kittery. We all unload my belongings, into my small as hell dorm room. My mother puts a on few finishing touches in the cleaning department. Windex, Lysol what have you.

I follow them out to the parking lot. And wave goodbye. Goodbye, to the only life I've ever known. Well, in reality. My father pulls my mother from her death grip around my neck. I hi five, Chance. My father grabs my shoulders, he whispers in my ear. " Go get um boy."

Refuse to Sink

My first couple of days alone here I ponder getting a shrink, while I'm in the city. Become a true New Yorker. But decide against it automatically.

My classes begin in a couple days, so I decide to get the lay of the land. Go to the bookstore. Meet some Teachers. And get to know where the lunch room is. I am starving. My feet feel heavy, my back aches from carrying this back pack full of books, for a good half mile. I am not sure why I'll need a algebra AP book. And what kind of Music major, needs to learn statistics? Pre-recs, you gotta love 'em. I think, as I shake the sweat off my head. I hear the school band and a commotion in the square. I guess there is going to be a concert? I look up and see a yellow printed sign, posted on one of the light post. John Mayer. Freaking John Mayer. How Ironic. How cruel. How awful. I miss Grace Anne immediately.

I decide, this is a concert I will skip. Because I am sure I wouldn't make it through, without seeing her face in every song and imagine her smile during her favorites. Turning to go back to my stale dormitory. I find myself crowded, in a mass of people. I am pushing and shoving (gently I'm not trying to hurt anyone.) Never the less; I am persistent to get out of here.

"Hello. Do you know what's going on down there?" I hear faintly from behind me. Hoping that someone else, would answer her burning question. "Hello??" she questioned.

"No, but I think maybe its John Mayer." I reply without looking back.

"Really I love him!" the young girl screams. I get a feeling inside my stomach, as if it just exploded.

My ears burn, my eyes feel like they will surely pop out of socket. My hands shake and before I can stop it, my torso turns in her direction. My body spins around as if on an axle. I am face to face with her. Grace Anne. It is her. I blink twice, wiping my eyes. I cannot talk. I am frozen. Oh no not again. Anchor snap out of it!

She stares at me. I stare at her. I cannot believe, what I am seeing. We both stop, dead in our tracks. I can feel my body swaying back and forth. I begin to fear I may pass out, or puke. People are circling around us. Pushing and shoving us together. Before we could prevent it, we are standing so close; I can smell her hair. Melon and flowers. Its the same smell. She breaks the silence.

" Hi, my name is Grace Anne, and yours would be?"

I feel the breath being stripped from my lungs, yet again. This time

D. C. Garriott

I don't have anyone to speak for me. So I desperately fight against it.

"Anchor. My name is Anchor. Yes I know its weird, but I am very nice, despite my weirdness." I smile widely, remembering Aria.

"Wanna stay with me and watch the concert." she questions, with that familiar twinkle in her eyes. "I don't know many people from here. And you seem very interesting for some reason." She winks, grabbing my sweaty hand.

And that was it. I found Grace. It was love at first sight, again. I spent the rest of that year convincing her, that I was the man of her dreams. She agreed to marry me, again. We now have a three year old little boy name AJ. Plus, one on the way. We reside in the upper east side of New York City. I did graduate from NYC and now I compose music for Broadway. My lovely Grace is moving up the ladder, at Central Park. And for my family. They are better than ever and very excited about their grandson.

I never told anyone about my "Dream life." I figure, it was meant for my eyes only. To guide me to where I am today. I no longer have dreams of lives left to live. And Thank God for that!

Grace Anne and I did make it to Paris. Our wedding, was just as I remembered it.

I found her, I found my dad. I found myself.

THE END.

Acknowledgments

I would like to thank my family. My husband Jason who through all his aggravation with this process, is still proud to call me his wife. And to my mother Wynna, for giving birth to a legend. I kid. I kid. I love you mom! Thank you for always believing in me! A special Thanks to Jackie Clifford. And I would like to thank Frank Hall, at Hydrapublications, for being so honest it changed my life! And lastly. I would like to thank God. Because without him. I wouldn't have it in me to do what I do!

D.C Garriott

D.C Garriott's Other book:
She Crossed The Line: Is available on line and in E book form!

Made in the USA
San Bernardino, CA
05 February 2015